RAIDING THE FORGOTTEN DERELICT

THE FORGOTTEN PLANET

KATE MACLEOD

CHAPTER 1

I t had taken more than twelve days of hiking and twelve nights of camping out under the stars for Lafayette Eloi and her father Pascal to get from her home village near the heart of the Great Grassy Sea to this jungle that had been the center of his work for months and months.

Twelve days of following the dirt track that ran first between fields of crops that were familiar to Lafayette.

Then past fields of crops that were less familiar to her, as they left rows of root vegetables behind in favor of grains. She had known the flour her momma had made pan bread from had come from ground-up grain, of course, but seeing the actual stalks bowing under the weight of their growing heads and dancing in the breezes was a new experience for her.

Then those fields of grain became fields of wild grasses, dry tufts of hardy but inedible plants that she had discovered—belatedly—had leaves that cut like knives.

Still, they were fields. And fields were familiar. Her world was a flat disc around her until it touched the blue of the sky. And at night the stars glittered so bright and heavy, they always looked like she could reach out and pluck one down if she just stretched out her hand.

Of course, she wasn't a kid anymore. She was nearly an adult now. She'd stopped believing that was *literally* true years ago. But the image still hung with her.

But each night her father had told her stories of the jungle they were heading to. He told her about trees. Not just a single tree, like the one that towered over the commons in the center of her home village, but more trees than anyone could possibly count.

And under the trees were plants like nothing she had ever seen, plants with wide fronds that caught the rain that managed to trickle down through the heavy canopy of the trees above.

She hadn't quite been able to imagine that. But once they reached the outskirts of the jungle on the thirteenth day, she wasn't completely surprised. She could put his stories into context now.

She really couldn't see the sun by day or more than a glimpse or two of the stars by night. And those trees really were tall, taller than she'd been able to imagine. It was so dark on the forest floor in most places that it was like being indoors all the time.

And his stories had prepared her for the noise of it all. There was a constant chattering of tiny mammals, twittering of birds, and yowling growls of larger things that, so far, had always been far off in the distance, lost among the trees.

He had warned her that the jungle was full of creatures, most of whom would prefer to avoid her—especially if she had her momma's dog Kora by her side—but some that required a bit of caution on her part.

And he had told her about the smells. Every plant had its own unique scent, and in the jungle it was like they were all competing to be the thing with the strongest scent. Brushing up against some of the plants would even leave her with one of those scents embedded in her clothes.

For whatever reason, it was always the smelliest of plants that had that effect. Every time.

But as Lafayette Eloi trudged along what she could only really hope was some sort of trail with her momma's dog Kora close by her side, she could name exactly one thing that her father had never warned her about or prepared her for.

The mud.

There was so much mud.

But it wasn't like normal mud at all. Or, at least, not like the mud Lafayette was used to. Back home, there would be mud after a heavy rain. But then the sun would rise higher in the sky, and soon even the mud in the shade of the buildings or of the tree in the center of the commons would be baked dry. The worst mud she had ever dealt with before had been after a rainy spring that had flooded the fields and destroyed that year's first planting.

Bad as that had been, even that had dried up after three days. There was just no way to stop the sun from baking it all back to its usual hard, dry state.

But the mud here? Here, where the trees held back all but the most stubborn of sunbeams?

Lafayette had real doubts this mud ever dried at all. It was always here, wet and deep.

Worse, it smelled like a lot of things had died in it, too. It smelled more strongly of rotting plants than the compost pile at the village back home had after that lazy waste of space Pierre had been the one on its duty roster for a week.

And more than once crossing the jungle mud, Lafayette had stepped down on something that had snapped under her boot. Not like a stick would snap, though.

No, she was pretty sure they had been bones. Something had gotten caught in the sucking stench of mud and had never gotten out again.

As she held onto a low-hanging tree branch to leverage her own stuck boot out of yet another deeper sink hole hidden in the mud, Lafayette had no problem imagining how that had happened.

Or imagining it maybe happening to her.

"Lafayette?" Kora said.

Which could mean lots of things, as it was the only world that Kora *could* say. Which was more than a normal dog could, but it was still really annoying how much work she had to do to figure out what the dog meant this time. She was busy.

Plus, it still stabbed at her heart just to look at the dog. The long red hair that had been turning to gray at almost exactly the same rate as Lafayette's momma's hair was growing in strawberry-colored again. The tail that had drooped for most of the last year was a tight curl once more, rolling back on itself in a tight spiral that stood tall over her hindquarters.

That change back to her youthful appearance and the accompanying rollback of her energy to her puppy days both were somehow harder for Lafayette to deal with than the fact that most of Kora's body had been replaced by bits of things her father had scavenged from Lafayette had no idea where. It was technology that no one in her village had seen before.

It had saved Kora's heart from giving out, and it was keeping her alive even now.

But Lafayette had to work not to hate the dog for living when her momma hadn't been so lucky. Or hating her father for not getting home in time to do anything for her momma.

Even if it was true what he said, that he couldn't have done anything for her even if he had been there.

He still should've been there. It shouldn't have been Lafayette all on her own as her mother faded away before her eyes.

"Lafayette?" Kora said again, more plaintively than before.

"I'm fine, Kora," Lafayette said between gritted teeth as she pulled at her foot to get it out of the mud. It came free with a suddenness that would've sent her into a face-plant right into the expanse of smelly, thick mud in front of her if she hadn't been holding onto that branch.

Like it had the first time she had gotten stuck. Lafayette took pride in only making a mistake one time. She knew how to adjust.

She clambered up onto a drier hillock of tufty plants that weren't exactly grass. Her father had said they were a type of reed, but that hadn't meant much to her either. Still, she had sketched the first tuft she had seen carefully into her journal and written "reed" beside it in her neatest script.

She only needed to be told what something was just one time either. She made a point of learning things.

"Lafayette?" Kora said yet again.

"I just need a minute to check the map," Lafayette said, although mostly she just needed to rest for a moment. Trying to wade through barely viscous mud was hard work. She was better at it now than she'd been when she and her father had first entered the jungle, but even so, her thighs and calves were aching so badly it was like they were screaming at her.

Lafayette pulled her satchel around to her lap, then dug out her journal. She had copied her father's map onto one of the pages, then marked that page with a bit of string. She turned to it now and consulted the drawing, then looked around at the jungle.

It was as dense as ever. She could see maybe five or six tree-layers in, and then it all became a wash of dark green, impenetrable to her eyes.

It was worse than being indoors, actually. Indoors at home, the windows and doors were always open when the weather was fair. But there was nothing she could do here to let in more sunlight or even a bit of the fresh breeze she could see tousling the treetops far above her.

She traced the path she had followed so far and was pretty sure she knew how far along it she was. But just to be sure, she took out the little handheld device her father had left with her. It was just a featureless metal disc, not even a shiny one.

It was also only the size of the palm of her hand, but she had to rest it flat on her palm to use it. She could curl her fingers around the edges a little, but not quite enough for it to feel secure.

She really didn't want to think about what she'd do if she dropped it in the mud.

When her father had given her this device on their first night camping in the jungle, it had looked as strange to her as the parts that made up Kora's body. But since then, she had gotten very familiar with it.

She stood up carefully, with both of her feet planted firmly on solid ground. Then she opened her hand and lifted it higher, so that the device on her palm was close to her eye level.

She aimed it towards where she thought the high ridge to the north was, the one they had climbed over to get into the jungle after leaving the grasslands behind.

The device in her hand beeped pretty strongly, but she adjusted her position until it was stronger still, and a green light flashed in its still featureless center.

Then a tracery of shapes were suddenly illuminated on its dull metallic surface. They were like letters made out of light, and they always looked like they were hovering over the top of the disc rather than inside or on the surface of the disc. But her attempts to poke them with her fingertip had never disrupted their shapes.

They were ghostly and creepy, but she had gotten used to them.

She had even started to recognize the repeating patterns of their shapes. Her father had said they were numerals, and she supposed that was true. There were only ten of them, and any of the ten could appear in any of the positions of the numbers the device showed her.

Not even her father knew what the sequence was, which digit meant one and which meant ten. He just showed her how to compare what was on the disc with what he had checked her copying of when she had drawn the map from his journal into her own. When the sequences matched, she was in the correct position.

But she always had to check both the ridge to the north and then the other location that was always due east from where she was. So she closed her hand over the disc again, watching her feet carefully as she shifted her position ninety degrees to her right. Then, when she was sure her feet were planted, she opened her hand and repeated the same small adjustments in her position until the light on the disc went green and the second string of strange digits were displayed.

"It's not much further now," she said as she tucked both the disc and her journal back in her satchel.

Of course, she had no way of knowing that for sure. All she knew was that she wasn't where the location on her map—the place she was searching for—was, yet.

But she was starting to get a gut sense of what the disc was trying to tell her.

As much as she was getting more confident in trusting that gut, she would still really prefer her gut would explain things clearly so that her brain could understand. She hated not really knowing.

But after finding the first seven marked locations on the map over the previous days, she didn't really expect to have any trouble finding the eighth. It was a little further west than the others, because she had started with the locations closest to her father's campsite, but that just meant a little more walking.

Through the mud.

With a sigh, Lafayette made sure her satchel was still securely slung across her shoulders. Then she put her first boot into the mud on the far side of the hillock and soldiered on through the jungle.

In search, just like her father was, of ancient artifacts. Like the disc in her satchel. And like the parts that had kept her momma's dog alive after her momma was dead and gone.

CHAPTER 2

Two hours of hiking later, Lafayette was starting to question whether she should really be trusting her gut.

On the upside, she had left the mud mostly behind. She was on slightly higher ground now. Higher and dryer. It was thick with the smelliest of the many plants she had encountered so far in the jungle—a plant with leafy fronds of a green so dark it bordered on purple, fronds that oozed a thick sap that smelled like concentrated cat pee—but even that was preferable to the mud.

On the downside, she wasn't entirely sure where she was. Had she walked too far, or not far enough?

"Lafayette?" Kora said when Lafayette had stopped walking to dig once more in her satchel.

"I know I just checked our position, but I'm checking it again," Lafayette said. Even though she was talking to a dog, she *did* try to keep the irritation out of her voice. It wasn't Kora's fault that Lafayette was in a bad mood.

Lots of things weren't Kora's fault.

But constantly hearing her name in that plaintive, questioning tone was really the most irritating thing about being all alone in this jungle.

"Lafayette," Kora said.

Only this time, it wasn't a question. This time, it sounded like Kora was trying to give her a heads up.

"What is it?" Lafayette asked.

And looked up from her hands digging through her satchel. Only for a split second, but that split second had been enough.

The flap she been holding tucked out of the way under her elbow slipped free, slapping against her groping hand.

And the disc that she was sure she had been grasping firmly slipped out of her fingers.

It almost fell back into the satchel again.

Almost.

But it bounced off the rim of the bag and landed edge-first on her toe.

It was a fairly heavy device for its size, and the edges were pointy, if not quite razor sharp.

But it was an even more sturdy boot. It bounced off the capped toe without Lafayette really feeling it hit her.

Then it rolled away, disappearing into a thicket of those purply green stinky fronds.

"Great," Lafayette said, and immediately dove in after the disc. Who knew how long it would keep rolling? Or if it would turn left or right? If she lost sight of it, she might never find it again.

And if she didn't find it again, she'd never get back to camp before dark.

She was pretty sure she could find her way back to her father's campsite on her own. But not before dark. Not without checking her position on the way to be sure she wasn't going astray.

She would swear the jungle moved around whenever she wasn't looking at it. It wanted her to get lost.

It wanted her to be food for whatever those growly, yowling things were.

Even her father hadn't known what made those sounds. But that was only because he avoided them, and strongly urged her to do the same.

And the best way to do that was to get back to camp before dark.

Lafayette realized that her thoughts were whipping around in a vicious circle, but she just couldn't make them stop. It only got worse as she scrambled about on her hands and knees, pushing sappy fronds away from her face and desperately searching for any sign of the dull metallic disc.

She was just starting to feel real despair when she saw it, laying on its side just beyond the last of the fronds in a rare patch of sunlight.

Lafayette lunged for it. She felt her fingers brush over its cool surface, then grasp around the edges until it was pressed tight against the palm of her hand.

She had it. It was safe. *She* was safe.

But then she felt something shifting beneath her. For a moment, she was confused. She wasn't crouching in mud; she was on solid ground. It wasn't rock, but it was dry and hard-packed.

And it was sliding away beneath her.

Lafayette yelped in alarm and tried to scramble back, but the ground was tipping faster than she could move. It was like she was sitting on an enormous plate that had been set too precariously on the edge of a table. It was tipping off the edge of the table like it was going to slide off onto the floor.

But all she could see were more trees. Where was she falling *to*?

Then it was like the plate snapped in the middle. Pretty much where Lafayette was, still trying to crab-crawl backwards. An awkward maneuver with the disc still clutched tightly in her right hand, but she was desperate to get back to where Kora waited on the far side of the thicket of plants.

The half that was just at Lafayette's fingertips behind her fell back flat, as it had been before.

But the half in front of her was now a sheer drop down into some sort of sinkhole.

For a moment she hovered there on the crumbling chasm where the two halves had once met.

But her fingertips couldn't grasp anything but dry dirt behind her. And then she was sliding, sliding down amongst an avalanche of dirt and broken, sappy fronds, down into the ground.

She landed hard, but once again she was grateful for the sturdy boots her father had given to her. They were laced high and tight to keep the mud from stealing them away from her. But those high sides also supported her ankles. So, yeah, she landed hard. But she didn't hurt anything. She was a little shaken, and she didn't much like that she had fallen so far from that rare shaft of sunlight that she was in nearly pitch darkness now.

But she was okay. She immediately stowed the disc safely inside her satchel.

"Lafayette?"

Wow. She had thought Kora had sounded plaintive before. She was downright bordering on neurosis now.

"I'm okay," she called up to the dog as she brushed dirt from the back of her pants. The heavy green fabric had felt too warm even in the grasslands when her father had given the pants to her, but like the boots, she was grateful for them now. They had kept many a stinging nettle or thorn from pricking her since coming to the jungle. And without them, sliding down that plate of hard-packed dirt would've surely left her with, at best, red, raw skin and torn clothing.

"I'm okay," she said again, mostly to herself that time. She needed to hear it.

But she wasn't sure if it was really true.

She blinked a few times, and watched as slowly what she had thought of as pitch blackness became more a gray of deep shadow. Not impenetrable.

But where she was standing was a mostly circular pit. A deep pit, about three times as deep as she was tall. The plate she had fallen in with was all smashed around her feet now, except those lighter bits that were still settling down in a thick cloud of dust around her.

She could see where it had calved from, above and behind her. It really had been like a plate that had slid off the surface. There was no fracture there she could reach and use to pull herself up.

The walls of the pit were sheer and tall. But they were also intensely crumbly. Even if she could force her fingers into a handhold, it just broke away into nothingness the minute she tried grasping it. Nothing was going to hold her weight.

And the pit was only a few meters across. But for her purposes, even that was too big. If it had been narrower, she could've braced her back against one side and her feet against the other and scrambled back out that way.

"Lafayette?" Kora called down again.

Lafayette could see her now, or at least her head. She was peering down into the hole.

"Get back from the edge!" Lafayette ordered her, and the dog rushed to comply.

But there was something odd about the way that head moved backwards. She didn't scramble back, like Lafayette had attempted to do before the plate of earth broke. No, it was more like she glided. Like Lafayette and the other kids did on skates in the winter when the irrigation canals froze.

Then Lafayette remembered something her father had told her, back when he'd first shown her what he had done with Kora. Lafayette hadn't really been listening at the time. She had still been upset about so many things, and the sudden change in Kora had been a lot to add to all those things.

But she remembered him showing her some of the parts he had assembled to keep Kora's heart pumping. He had replaced all of her internal organs with machine parts. He had stopped explaining when he had sensed that Lafayette wasn't so much curious as horrified.

But not before he had told her that the parts were too heavy for Kora's little doggy legs to tote about. So he had also installed a hovering mechanism.

Lafayette chewed at her lip. She only kind of understood what that might mean. And she'd mostly forgotten it because, once she got used to the sight of her momma's dog now being half made of metal, it had stopped seeming weird. Now the dog was just like a younger version of Kora, one that was wearing an awkward metal vest.

Certainly, she had never looked like she was hovering. Her father must have set it to be just enough for Kora's legs to handle the new weight, but not so much that she was suddenly able to bound up into the air or fly or anything.

But Lafayette was suddenly wildly curious if that was possible. If it was possible to make Kora fly.

If maybe even *she* could do it.

She had figured out how the disc worked. She knew how the fence protecting the campsite worked. She had learned a lot about the technology her father had been scavenging and tinkering with his entire adult life, and she had learned it all in just a few days.

More than that, she had learned how to figure things out now. What questions to ask herself that would lead to useful answers. Like questions about how Kora's hover disc worked and what more it could possibly do.

But it didn't matter now. Even if she could do it, she had no tools in her satchel. They were all back at camp.

And she was at the bottom of the hole, and Kora was at the top of it. And they were both effectively alone.

Lafayette looked around again, hoping that she had missed something in her first examination.

This was her eighth hole in the ground. Not that she'd fallen in and gotten trapped at the bottom of the others.

But that wasn't the only thing that was different about this hole.

No, this hole wasn't really like the others at all.

Despite the urgency of the situation, Lafayette felt a strong compulsion to carry on with the actual task her father had assigned her to do when he had left the camp on his own seven days before. She wouldn't take much time with it, but she really needed to record all she found so she could share it with him later.

So she sat down on the dirt, pulled out her journal, and sketched all the details of the hole she had fallen into.

The others had been craters, really. Places where bits of things had fallen from the sky with enough force to leave just such a hole. Lafayette had pages of drawings from those places, too. Most of the artifacts she had found there had been no more than the size of one of her knucklebones. Nothing the size of the disc. Nothing remotely useful.

But definitely metallic. Definitely not anything she'd ever find back home in the village.

This hole, on the other hand, wasn't a crater. She was sure her father would agree. It just didn't look like the others.

It had to be some sort of natural sinkhole. Not that she actually knew what was natural for a jungle. But her father would know.

After she had done a couple of sketches of the look of the exposed earth that formed the sides of the sinkhole, she dug through the dirt beneath her with her fingertips. There was nothing under the layer of dirt she had brought down with her but plant matter.

It had a drier smell than the plants that were rotting in the mud. It also felt more fibrous than the fronds she had crawled through moments before.

"Lafayette?" Kora called again.

"Hold on, Kora," Lafayette said as she dug through the dirt, finding more and more of the dried plants. They looked like the remains of some sort of vine, perhaps fallen from the higher branches of the trees above.

None of them were long enough to reach the top of the hole. Because she'd never be that lucky.

But that was okay. Lafayette knew how to make rope. Sure, she'd always worked from dried grass before.

But feeling the fibers of the dried vines in her hands, she had a feeling they were going to make an even stronger rope than the ones she had made back home.

She didn't need much. Just seven meters or so.

As she started to twist the fibers together, her hands falling into a familiar rhythm almost at once, she tried hard not to think about the sun. And how soon it would be setting.

She had to get back to camp before dark. She just had to.

CHAPTER 3

Twisting fibers into rope was slow work. When Lafayette had done it before back in her village, it had been one of the sorts of jobs that were done in the winter months. Everyone would gather around the fire in the meeting hall and spin, weave, carve, or any of a hundred other little bits of handcraft that their farming community needed to have done.

But it was also the time for sharing stories, for singing, for playing riddle games. Lafayette and her mother had never been an integral enough part of the village to be near the center of things, but even far from the fire Lafayette could hear the stories and laugh at the jokes or sing along with the familiar choruses of the old songs.

At the bottom of the pit, alone and in the growing dark, there was none of that to take her mind off the monotony of the chore.

And there was no way to make it happen faster. Not if she wanted the rope to be strong enough to hold her weight. Which, of course, she did.

The fibers were coarser than the dried grasses she was used to working with. While she was still sure this meant they'd be a stronger rope, they were also a lot rougher on her hands. Not sharp enough to cut like the bladed leaves of that other sort of jungle plant, but enough to leave the skin of her palms scraped and raw.

Which made it that much harder to focus on keeping the twisting going, keeping it smooth and even.

"Lafayette?" Kora called for probably the twentieth time.

"Still here. Still working," Lafayette assured her. Then she paused to stretch the muscles of her hand and examine the length of her rope.

She was nearly there. Maybe another meter, just to be sure.

But it was also getting darker.

It was hard to tell just how much darker. As difficult as it was to judge the height of the sun anywhere under the dense canopy of the treetops, it was that much more difficult to do it while sitting at the bottom of a hole.

But it was definitely late afternoon.

Above her, she could hear Kora pacing again. Back and forth, back and forth, but never far from the lip of the hole. She had done that all her life when she was anxious, usually when Lafayette's momma was seeing someone in their home, someone who was nervous around dogs. Then Kora would have to stay home alone with Lafayette.

Neither of them had liked that arrangement much. And it was always a relief to both of them when Momma came back home.

Kora hadn't paced in that nervous way once since Momma had died. But she was doing it now.

It felt weird, knowing that this time Kora was anxiously pacing because it was Lafayette she was desperate to be closer to.

Lafayette didn't quite get another meter onto the rope. Not because of the growing darkness, but because she'd run out of dried vines on the bottom of the hole. She played the length out in her hands with a frown, then dug through the dusty top layer all over the bottom of the hole. But there was nothing else to work with.

What she had was going to have to be enough.

She stood up and played the rope through her hands again, this time pulling on it repeatedly to test its strength.

She was sure it would be strong enough. She just wasn't sure if it would be long enough.

"Kora!" she called up, and the dog poked her head over the side so quickly it was like she had just been waiting to hear her voice. "I need you to catch this rope. Can you do that for me? Can you catch this rope when I toss it up?"

"Lafayette!" Kora said eagerly.

That sounded like a yes.

Lafayette's first toss was really rather pathetic. The end of the rope didn't even make it halfway up to where Kora leaned in, mouth open, waiting for it.

"Hold on," Lafayette mumbled. She was going to have to sacrifice a little bit of the length, even though she still wasn't sure she had enough to spare. But she made a knot as close to the end as she could, pulling it tight before knotting it again. After the third time, she had a knot about the size of her fist, heavier than the rest of the rope.

"Okay, here it comes," she said, and tossed the knot up to Kora.

Kora lunged so far out over the hole that Lafayette caught herself squeaking in alarm, scrambling back in case that very heavy dog was about to come down right on her head.

But Kora hovered back noiselessly, the rope gripped firmly in her jaws.

"Good job, girl!" Lafayette said.

Kora made a happy sound, but clearly she didn't dare open her mouth to actually answer.

The bottom of the rope ended at a point about level with Lafayette's shoulders. So the first bit of the climb was going to be the hardest, but the dirt on the sides of the hole on the bottom looked harder packed than on the top edge. Which looked like it was still ready to crumble at any moment.

Lafayette gave the rope an experimental tug. Kora held it firm. The rope itself held firm.

There was nothing left to do but start climbing.

Lafayette grasped the rope in both of her hands, ignoring the protest from her already abused palms. But as soon as she lifted her feet off the ground to kick out towards the side of the hole, she felt Kora sliding forward. Kora whimpered in alarm, but Lafayette had already let go.

Let go and scrambled back to the far side of the hole. The image of that dog falling down on top of her was too, too vivid in her mind's eye.

But Kora remained where she was, the knotted rope in her mouth.

"I need more stability on your end," Lafayette said, chewing on her lip as she pondered her options. "There are trees around you, but none close enough to help. Not with the amount of rope we have, at any rate. And I can't make more."

Kora made an inarticulate sound.

"No, even if you could find more of the vines for me, and even if the vines you found were dry enough for me to work with, time is running out. We have to work with what we have."

But how?

Kora made another inarticulate sound. Then she shook her head, sending a ripple down the length of rope. Clearly, she wanted Lafayette to hurry up.

"Kora," Lafayette said as a sudden thought struck her. "You have a hover disc in your belly. My father put it in you because without it your core would be too heavy for your legs, right?"

Kora grunted. It sounded like she was agreeing.

"Right, and I think you've been using it just now every time you get close to the edge. You're letting yourself hover a little extra to keep from crumbling the edge under your own weight. To keep from falling down on top of me. That's why I could pull you so easily when I tried to climb just now. Right?"

Kora grunted again.

"Right," Lafayette said, really hoping that she wasn't deluding herself about how much the two of them were having a conversation, a meaningful exchange of information. She really needed Kora to understand just now. "What I need you to do, Kora, is to stop hovering. The weight of your core without your hover disc functioning is like a rock. Like a rock that weighs twice what you think it will. That's going to anchor me just fine."

Kora made another sound halfway between a grunt and a happy little bark. Then she snapped her jaws tight around the rope again, as if she had almost let it slip out of her grasp.

"Okay," Lafayette said, and stepped forward to grab the rope again.

"I'm going to let you pull me until I feel you anchor down. Then I'll climb out myself. Make sure you're far enough away from the edge first, all right?"

Kora just shook her head, sending another ripple down the rope. Lafayette gripped it tighter, then put one foot on the side of the hole, ready to keep up with the speed of the pulling rope as soon as it got started.

The rope went just the tiniest bit slack for a moment, but then snapped tight again as Kora's head disappeared from the edge of the hole. She was backing up, but so smoothly and silently that Lafayette doubted she was actually using her legs at all.

Just how much control of the hover disc did she have with her little doggy brain?

But before Lafayette could more than wonder at the question, the rope in her hands started to tug up and away from her. She held it tight, leaning her weight on her front foot before finally bringing the other up off the bottom of the hole and started a sort of walking motion up the side of the hole.

It was really, really awkward. Her boots kept slipping on the loose dirt, sending cascades down to the bottom of the hole below her. But the rope continued to tug her up at a slow but steady pace.

Then it stopped moving. That part was sudden and far from silent. Apparently, Kora had just switched off power to her hover disc entirely. Lafayette could hear Kora's body impact with the ground with a thunk.

Lafayette took a deep breath, then started climbing hand over hand, foot after foot, up the crumbling side of the hole and the even more crumbling lip. She sent so much dirt skittering down the hole behind her, clouds of it covered her body, clinging to her sweaty skin and coating every follicle of her hair.

Then her vertical climb became horizontal, and she let go of the rope and continued crawling forward on her hands and knees until she reached the point where Kora had planted herself.

Only when Lafayette had buried both of her hands in the dog's red fur and scratched all around the dog's ears in happy thanks did Kora finally spit out the knotted end of the rope and look up at her with her tongue lolling out of the side of her mouth.

"I bet you're thirsty," Lafayette said. As tired as she was, she forced herself to sit up then take the canteen out of its pouch on the side of her satchel. She pulled out a collapsible bowl and opened it up before pouring half of the canteen's contents into it.

Kora drank her share in great thirsty gulps. Lafayette sipped at hers. She started to brush at the buns of her hair, but after even the fifth hit was still sending out a cloud of dust that seemed in no way diminished since the first, she decided that her hair would have to wait until she got back to camp.

Back to camp.

"Time to go, girl," she said to Kora as she put the bowl and canteen away, then pushed herself up onto her feet. It wasn't as dark on the surface as it had been down at the bottom of the hole, but it was still darker than she'd like it to be.

And she was so very far from camp.

Lafayette started off at a jog, Kora matching her pace with ease. But that only lasted until she reached the first patch of mud.

Luckily, because she was coming back the way she had gone, she already knew where the driest paths were. Even if she hadn't quite remembered, the mud was so thick it had barely filled in the footprints she had left hours before.

But that also meant that it was no drier than before. As much as she longed to run, the pull of all that wet earth on her boots was simply too strong. The mud was too deep. It was a slog.

She wished she had a hover disc like Kora. Then she could just glide over the top of it.

Although Kora was up to her hips in it herself. Lafayette suspected that was a gesture of solidarity. She always matched Lafayette's pace, no matter how fast or how slow she was going. But she never once got bogged down.

As Lafayette struggled through the mud, she started to worry about the growing darkness. Even aside from being caught out so very far from camp, it was getting dark enough now that she was starting to worry she'd lose sight of her footprints. Then she'd have to keep stopping and checking her position. That was going to slow her down even more, just when she especially needed to be fast.

Then she saw something twinkling up ahead of her. For the briefest of moments she thought she was seeing the one thing she wanted most to see in the world: not just the campsite, but the campsite with her father in it, waiting for her, shining all the lights out into the forest to show her the way back.

But the twinkles were too small, and the color all wrong for the electric lights her father had dozens of. Those shone with a bluish-white light, like tiny but bright stars you could hold in your hands.

What Lafayette was seeing now was something else. Something greenish-yellow. Dimmer.

But as she trudged on through the mud, she realized she was seeing more of those lights than her father had in the camp. Lots more. There were hundreds of them. But they weren't sitting on the ground or hanging from the branches of the trees. They were in motion, floating around in lazy loops, blinking on and off again before they could quite describe an entire circle.

Insects. They were insects. Her father had told her about these things, although he had told her that the lights in the camp would drive them away. Apparently, they didn't like the competition.

Then Lafayette reached the end of the mud pit and could once more walk and jog through the dense foliage. But she knew she was close to camp now. She could see so many places were she had broken fronds and even branches as she had passed over the last eight days.

Which was a good thing. The sounds of the jungle around her were changing. The birds and droning insects of day were fading away, and the skittering creatures of the night were starting up their furtive little bursts of sound under a chorus of a different group of droning insects.

She didn't hear the growly yowling yet. The screeches of the animals she very much didn't want to see any closer. Not yet. But she knew she would soon.

Then she saw the outline of the tent itself, standing apart from the other trees in the closest thing to a clearing that her father had ever found in his many trips into this jungle.

The sight of the camp was heartening, but Lafayette couldn't help feeling a stab of disappointment. Even if it had mostly been a mirage, the sight of the camp lit up as her father waited for her had been so strong in her mind, she couldn't help feeling cheated by this second best version.

Now she'd have to fire up the perimeter fence and turn on all the lights herself. She would be the one waiting, looking out at the surrounding trees, watching for any sign of her father returning.

He said it would be twelve days at the most. This nightfall made eight. He wasn't late yet.

But four more days of waiting still felt like more than Lafayette could take.

"Come on," she said to Kora, who was trotting along at her side as they approached the camp under the light of the first stars. "Let's get something to eat. I think we both deserve a treat after that day, don't you?"

Kora barked in nonverbal agreement. Whatever else she may or may not have understood, Kora had always known the word "treat."

CHAPTER 4

Although it hadn't rained all day where Lafayette and Kora had been, the camp had gotten a good dousing at some point. The barrel at the bottom of the rain collector array was three-quarters full.

Which was great, since after falling down and climbing back out of that hole, Lafayette really needed a bath.

But first she coaxed the fire back to life and put a kettle over the coals to boil enough water to reconstitute her dinner. She grabbed the first envelope in the box and tore it open, then dumped the contents into her camp bowl without so much as glancing at the label. At this point, she was sick to death of all the options. One soup or stew was pretty much the same as any other.

She would kill for a slice of bread. Let alone for one of her momma's ginger cakes.

Her mouth started to water before she got that thought firmly out of her mind. No good would come from fantasizing about what she couldn't have. Besides, she had work to do.

While she waited for the water in the kettle to come to a boil, she measured out a bit of the food paste that was all Kora needed to maintain her remaining living tissue. It smelled like fermented beans, not necessarily unappetizing, but definitely too strong a smell for Lafayette to handle for long. Luckily, Kora always licked it all up in three or four passes, then settled into her usual spot by the fire to lick what remained off her lips for what always seemed like hours.

It kept her happy.

The kettle whistled, and Lafayette wrapped a scrap of towel around the handle before lifting the metal implement off of the coals. She poured the first few dribbles carefully, then once the dehydrated stuff had drunk up enough liquid to lay quiet at the bottom of the bowl without spattering, she poured up to the usual line on the side of the bowl then left it to sit and cool for a few minutes.

She saw carrots emerging from the depths, then cubes of potatoes, and finally the bits of what she knew was meant to be beef, but really, really wasn't. But she was hungry, and it had calories. That was all that mattered at the moment.

"Kora, roll over," Lafayette said, turning her attention back to the dog.

"Lafayette!" Kora said happily, rolling onto her back to show Lafayette her belly.

Lafayette reached in like she was going to give Kora a belly rub, and Kora's palpable delight was the same as when she used to get belly rubs from Lafayette's momma. But there wasn't any belly to rub anymore. There was just that metallic core that contained whatever Lafayette's father had cobbled together to replace Kora's failing organs.

That, and the hover disc.

But also the power cell that kept it all running. Her father had told her there was really no reason why that cell should ever run down or fail in any way. But Lafayette checked it every night anyway.

There was no reason why her mother had run down and died. She had only been thirty-eight. But it had happened anyway.

Kora twisted this way and that on her back playfully, so it took Lafayette a moment to catch a glimpse of the power indicator by fire-light. But the green glow that meant it was in its optimal state was unmistakable.

"Good girl," Lafayette said, patting Kora's side. Kora sat back up at once and resumed licking at her own face.

Lafayette just shook her head in bemusement, then picked up her bowl of not quite beef stew and started spooning it in.

It warmed her belly. And the carrots were actually really good considering they had been freeze-dried who knows how many years ago then reconstituted in filtered rain water. They and the potatoes both tasted like they had been roasted in an oven before being turned into dried cubes in a dust of powdered broth.

She wished she had some mushrooms to add just to give the thin broth a little more flavor. But since coming to the jungle, while she had seen many kinds of fungi in a variety of shapes and colors, none of it had matched anything in her mother's botany journal.

Everything was so different here. Nothing in her mother's lore was helping Lafayette at all. She had brought all six of her mother's thick journals filled with her tiny but neatly legible writing and sketches with her, mostly because she didn't expect to ever return to the village again and hadn't wanted to leave them behind.

But she had also really thought they'd be useful, too. Some of the knowledge they contained were things her momma had already taught her, but a lot of it were things her momma had known but never shared. Page after page of botanical lore and medicinal knowledge.

And not a bit of it was useful here, in a place she knew her mother had come to more than once.

But she had always hated it here. Not that she had ever said so. Not that Lafayette's father had ever said so.

But they hadn't had to. Lafayette knew there was a reason her parents didn't live together anymore. Or hadn't, for years before her mother died.

And it hadn't been because they didn't love each other. They had just been *of* different worlds.

Lafayette scraped the last of the stew off the sides of her bowl, then licked it off her spoon as she looked around at the trees. It felt like they were hovering so close all around the camp. Looming. Like they could move closer or grow taller in the darkness.

She wasn't sure if she liked this place much more than her mother did.

But she really hadn't felt *of* the world of the village. Not after her mother died. Not even before her father had saved Kora's life by turning her into something the rest of the village hadn't wanted to have anything to do with.

Lafayette washed her bowl and spoon, then put them away in the box of cooking supplies where she had taken them from. Her father had stressed the importance of keeping the camp neat in case they needed to pack everything and flee in a hurry.

Lafayette didn't need to be told anything twice.

Although sometimes she resented not being told something just once. Like why they would ever need to flee in a hurry. But her father had brushed off that question as brusquely as he had all the others he simply wasn't going to answer.

Like where he was, just at that moment. All Lafayette knew was that he was east of the camp, and would be there for another four days.

Her father had said, "At the most. It will be twelve days at the most." He had said *that* more than once.

But Lafayette had heard similar from him every time he had left after visiting the village. He would promise to be back in four months, or two years, or any number at all, really. And after he'd disappeared over the horizon, her momma would always turn to her and give her that sad yet pointed look.

She had never said it out loud, but Lafayette had worked out what that look had meant from a very young age. It meant that her father really thought he'd be back in whatever amount of time he'd just said. But Momma and Lafayette both knew that whatever he intended, the reality would be different.

And it was always longer. He never got back sooner.

Lafayette pushed those thoughts aside as she stripped off her clothes, beating as much of the dirt out of them as she could before plunging them into the tub she had filled for laundry.

Then she scrubbed herself using water from the other tub. It wasn't quite a bath—the tub was far too small for her to sit in—but it was soapy and warm. And it just felt better, being clean before she got into her sleeping shirt and shorts.

She washed and rinsed her clothes and hung them from a line close to the fire, then made a quick check of the perimeter fence. Like Kora's power cell, this was never supposed to fail. But, like with Kora's power cell, she always felt better if she checked it before getting into the tent for the night.

She could hear things moving just out of reach of the campfire, skittering through the underbrush or rustling through the lower-hanging branches of the trees. But they all sounded like small creatures. They were clearly more frightened than she was.

But not of her. No, what frightened them was more likely to be the growling, yowling things.

She wasn't hearing any of them that night, though. At least, not yet. There was no hint of light to the west where the sun had set, but it was still early for all that.

Lafayette checked the last perimeter fence post, but everything was green on the panel. The fence was live. The fence would protect her.

Kora looked like she'd fallen asleep by the fire, but when Lafayette ducked inside the tent, Kora immediately got to her feet and padded after her.

Lafayette zipped the flap shut behind the dog, then sat on the little rug her father had spread on the ground in front of his travel desk. It was like a sloped box on little legs that could be folded flat against its bottom when stowed on the hover cart with the rest of the gear. With the legs extended, it was just tall enough for Lafayette to fit her crossed legs beneath it.

She lifted the cover and dug through the couple of journals her father had left behind for her use. First, she double checked his version of the map again, pulling out her own journal from her satchel and reviewing where she and Kora had gone that day.

Not an artifact site. Just a random indentation in the ground. Which, she knew her father would tell her, didn't mean it had been a waste of time. It had looked worth checking out, and she had checked it out.

She made a notation in her father's journal that the sinkhole had been a natural formation, then closed that journal and stowed it away inside the box again.

But then she pulled out the green canvas-covered journal of her father's. This she opened up under the light that hung from the tent support above her and smoothed down the first of the pages. Unlike the blank paper of the other journals, the pages in this book had been printed with a grid pattern before they had come into her father's possession. His writing and diagrams were on top of those grid lines.

She hadn't looked much at this book after he'd told her what it was, but she was looking at it now. The diagrams were meant to be telling her all about the machine parts her father had used to fix Kora. Schematics, her father had called them.

Lafayette examined schematic after schematic, reading the labels in her father's blocky printing, and trying to follow what the parts meant.

If she studied this book, all of it, and really understood it, she just knew she could alter Kora's hover disc. Then Kora could be flying around like those light insects that zoomed among the trees, far out of sight from the camp.

But after an hour of careful study, Lafayette didn't feel like she'd learned anything. All she had was more questions than she'd had before she started. There were words she didn't know, and the pattern that must be there tying all of these things together conceptually just eluded Lafayette.

Finally, she gave up with a sigh, put out the lights, and climbed into the sleeping bag.

It was mechanical, what was in that journal. That was the trouble. Mechanical, electrical, chemical even. All fields of study worlds away from what she had learned in the village.

Even the things her momma had taught her, things that her momma insisted had to be their secret and never shared with the rest of the village, those things had been relatable to the world around Lafayette. Plants and animals and medicines and things. Even things she'd never seen with her own eyes, like the structure of the cells that made up everything, were still things she could imagine.

Lafayette sensed her mind longing to sink into a useless melancholy, and forced it to stop. No sinking. Not today.

Today, she had gotten herself out of a bad situation. She had *thought* her way out. She had made a plan that had worked, and it had worked because she had implemented it using what she had and what she knew.

She wasn't useless.

She was just… more alone than she had ever been before.

Lafayette had barely formed the image of her momma in her mind —as much as she didn't want to, didn't want to risk the emotional overload that would follow that line of thought—when, as if she had sensed what was going on inside Lafayette's mind and soul, Kora got up from where she had settled near the tent door and came over to Lafayette's side. She curled up against Lafayette's belly, resting her warm snout on the open palm of Lafayette's hand.

Lafayette lay stiffly, as if frozen in shock, for several long minutes.

Kora was her momma's dog. Kora slept in her momma's bed. Kora had never cuddled with Lafayette, ever.

But she was cuddling her now.

Kora blew out a sad doggy sigh, and Lafayette slipped her other arm around Kora's strangely warm metal core, hugging her tight.

She was just wondering if there was something in her father's green covered journal that would explain that warmth when the droning of the night insects and the evenness of Kora's breathing just lulled her to sleep.

CHAPTER 5

The forest around her was still darkly gray when Lafayette put on her now-dry clothing, pulled on her boots, and slung her satchel over her shoulder to head out of camp once more.

There was only one depression on the map she had copied from her father's journal left for her to check. But it was the one furthest from camp.

At least it was almost due south from the camp. The land in that direction was hillier, but the mud only lurked in the deeper hollows. If she could pick a trail that stuck to the higher ground and skirted around the valleys, she would have an easier hike today.

Kora bounded along beside her with her usual early morning energy. She would be plodding as steadily as Lafayette was already doing by lunchtime. But for now her ears were perked up and her nose was constantly sniffing the air, turning her head at this scent or that.

But she was too disciplined to leave Lafayette's side. Sometimes she made a lamenting little whine when she had to turn away from something she was particularly tempted to explore further, but she never let herself be lured away.

Lafayette was glad for her company. This was the ninth day she had been otherwise completely alone. It wasn't something that she was used to.

Although, she thought as she walked with her usual long-striding rhythm, on the other hand, she kind of was. As much as she hadn't actually been born there, she didn't have any memories before the time she and her mother had moved into the hut left vacant by the previous medicine woman's death. She couldn't recall a home that didn't smell of herbs and poultices, where she slept every night under the rafters hung with drying bunches of plants.

Her mother had quickly found a place in that community. Her skills had been desperately needed, especially those first few years when the trade routes from the capital had become impassable, first because of bandits and later because of the two bad winters when all the rivers and streams overran their banks and washed out the bridges.

Lafayette couldn't remember those times, either. No, by the time her memories began, her mother was already vital to the community.

But that hut stood apart from all the others. And so Lafayette had grown up, just a little apart from all the others.

No one had ever been mean to her or anything. They just hadn't been friendly either. They had gathered around when her mother had fallen ill, and while they couldn't do a thing to make her mother well, they had at least made sure that Lafayette was still fed. That her home fire always had fuel to burn.

But her sorrow was her own. She had no one to share it with.

Now she truly was alone. But aside from a niggle of fear that never quite left the back of her mind—a fear of what could happen to her when there was no one around to even know she needed help—she mainly felt actually quite comfortable with her solitude. It was like a pressure she hadn't even known had been there her entire life had just been lifted.

She didn't have to make sure the doors and windows were closed before she took out her journals, for one. She could sit with the tent door open to catch the breezes as she perused all the journals her father had left behind. She could sit outside in the middle of the day and look at her momma's beautiful illustrations of fungi and other plants in the full light of the sun, something she'd never been able to do before.

Well, what sunlight she could find through the tree cover. The camp was in the largest clearing her father could find, but the gap in the trees overhead wasn't particularly generous. More like a natural chimney to let the smoke from the campfire out.

And it was even darker where she was now, hiking with Kora. The ground was hillier, but the jungle was denser the further south they walked. Checking her position was trickier as well. The north position was still north of where she was, since it was lining up to a point at the ridge overlooking the jungle she was in.

But the point that had been to her east all day yesterday was moving behind her as she walked, getting more and more northward. Because what she was lining up with to check that position wasn't at the eastern ridge that overlooked the jungle. Those rocky peaks had been taller and steeper, too treacherous for her father to put a beacon there.

No, the beacon for that position was the dead center of the bowl-like valley that contained the entire jungle. From the northern ridge, it almost looked like some giant had filled that bowl with living green, as if trees had a liquid form. They didn't extend past the rocky ridges in any direction, her father had told her. They just sat there, like they were confined to that bowl.

But they certainly flourished inside the bowl, a fact that Lafayette was well aware of as she skirted around yet another impenetrable thicket of undergrowth to find an easier path that still led her south.

Lafayette reached her destination at almost noon precisely. She stood at the lip of the little crater for a moment, relieved to once again be looking at an array of objects to be cataloged and sketched and not another natural sinkhole that would try its best to trap her.

Then she shared a little water with Kora and ate a ration bar herself. She always felt a little guilty eating lunch without sharing with Kora, but Kora only needed a little of that special paste, and only once a day. And she didn't seem to mind. She just took the opportunity while Lafayette was stationary and chewing to finally explore a few of the closer smells.

Or maybe she already knew that the ration bar was no real treat. It tasted like peanut butter and dust with a lingering acrid aftertaste. As much as it was far too crumbly for something that was meant to be eaten out of the package, it also stuck to her teeth like undercooked candy. Which made that aftertaste really linger.

Lafayette took one last swallow from her canteen to try to clear her mouth as much as possible. Then she took out her journal and got to work.

The first step was to draw everything as she saw it, the position and relative size of everything. A tree had fallen over near the lip of the crater, and perched on the side of the dying trunk, she had the perfect view for that task. It was wide enough for her to sit cross-legged without worry of falling off, and she spread her journal open on her knee as she sketched.

Her father had been impressed when he had looked at Lafayette's drawings, the ones she had done of the layout of her mother's garden back in the village. But that compliment had actually irked Lafayette more than a little. She knew that he only knew how to draw this way because her momma had taught him scale and perspective back when they had been students together. But apparently he had forgotten.

Or he hadn't realized how much life had gone by in all those months and years he had been away, hunting for more bits from the past.

Bits like the things Lafayette was drawing now. Once she had a couple of good sketches of the entire bottom of the crater, she got down from the tree trunk and picked her way down. The sides of the crater were smooth, dry dirt, sloping gently down to the bottom. Unlike the sinkhole, this crater had been here for untold years. Even her father didn't know for sure, although he told her his best guess for everything he'd found in this jungle so far was at least a thousand years.

But, he had made very clear, that was just a guess.

Lafayette couldn't quite wrap her head around that number. So she just pressed on with what she could do. Which was sketch and catalog what she found.

There were six distinct objects visible at the bottom of the crater.

They were half covered with the light dirt that had blown down into the hole, but they still gleamed in what sunbeams reached them. They were metal of some sort. Perhaps she would find something useful, like the disc that helped her find her position in the jungle.

But more likely it was more broken pieces of things too mysterious for Lafayette to even guess at. She had filled a crate with them back at the camp: metal shards with sharp edges, blackened rings that were often partially crushed out of their true round shape, weird bendy pieces like metallic elbows.

She didn't know what any of it was for. But she hoped when her father saw it all, he could identify at least some of it. That something she had gathered would be of some use in his work.

After she'd sketched all six pieces in situ, she took a little brush out of her satchel and gently cleared the dirt away from each piece one at a time. There was always the chance that something that looked small and worthless on the surface was only one protruding part of some larger, more interesting thing.

But today was not her lucky day. All she had when she was done was six more pieces of broken tech to put in her satchel.

They didn't even look like they wanted to fit together.

Wherever her father had found the parts that he had used to build Kora's new body, it hadn't been at the bottom of a crater. But that really shouldn't be surprising. Her father had told her these things had fallen out of the sky, streaking on fire like a shooting star before hitting the ground with immense force.

It was a miracle this much had survived, really.

But it really made her mind itch, wondering what her father was up to. He had assigned her nine depressions he had thought might be craters, and eight of them had been.

But while Lafayette was cataloging the contents of craters, her father was doing something else. Something so involved he couldn't even make it back to camp at night.

He had promised he was still inside the jungle valley, the same as Lafayette. But now that she had reached the furthest point on the map and was heading back, fully expecting to be back at camp safely before sundown, she *really* had to wonder what he was up to. Why he was gone all day and all night.

Where he was gone.

"Come, Kora," Lafayette called as she climbed back out of the crater. Kora emerged from a nearby thicket of tall grass, tail wagging as she trotted over to Lafayette's side. Lafayette gave her one last drink of water, took one herself, then the two of them headed north again.

It would be another evening alone with Kora. Eating another random envelope of dehydrated food. Putting labels on the new artifacts before adding them to the others in the crate. Updating her journal, then reading more of her father's.

But what really loomed over her was what she was going to do the next day. She had checked all the other depressions already. There was no more work left for her to do.

But she still had three more days to fill.

Maybe more than that, if her father was late.

And if there was one thing she'd always been able to rely on her father for, it was for being late.

She knew it was too soon to worry, but she just couldn't help it.

She wondered where he was.

CHAPTER 6

Lafayette spent the next two days entirely inside the confines of the camp. She pored over her father's journals, particularly the one with all the drawings on grids. The ones that explained Kora's artificial body.

By the end of the first day, she thought she might actually be understanding how it all fit together.

By lunchtime on the second day, she thought she was ready to try making one small adjustment.

"Kora, do you trust me?" she said to the dog as she shut the journal and stowed it away inside the desk.

"Lafayette!" Kora said eagerly, and rushed over to her.

Lafayette was pretty sure Kora thought they were going for a walk. Two days inside the perimeter fence had gone by in a flash for Lafayette, lost as she was inside those journals. But it had probably been pretty boring for the dog.

"Belly rubs," Lafayette said, and Kora immediately flopped over and let Lafayette see her belly.

There. That recessed notch just under Kora's right front armpit. It had looked like just part of where two parts joined to Lafayette before, but now she suspected it was actually a switch. Not on/off, but one that gradually shifted from one state to another as the piece of metal no larger than the head of a pin was moved from one side of the oval notch to the other.

Lafayette used the tip of her pencil to nudge it just a little further towards the middle of the notch.

"Okay, Kora. Stand up and try that out," she said.

Kora writhed a few times first, like she had an itchy spot on her back that she wanted to scratch on the ground first. Then she rolled over and got to her feet.

"Okay, try jumping," Lafayette said.

The dog just looked at her, tongue lolling out of the side of her mouth.

"Jump," Lafayette said again. Then she got to her feet and demonstrated.

"Lafayette!" Kora said, and leapt up into the air.

She immediately shot up, higher than Lafayette's head, so high that she collided with the roof of the tent before coming back down.

The look of confusion on the dog's face was funny, but Lafayette just managed not to laugh out loud.

"Come on. Let's go outside and try it," Lafayette said, and headed out the tent door to the center of the camp. Kora bounded after her, each of her bounds now longer and floatier than they had been before.

"Lafayette!" Kora said in palpable delight as she bounded around and around the camp. She jumped higher and higher, then bounded some more.

She couldn't quite fly, but she could definitely glide.

"Okay, Kora. Try standing still, now. You should be able to control it if you want to. Like you did when I climbed out of that hole," Lafayette said. But Kora kept bounding around the campsite, tail wagging emphatically. "Kora! Down!" Lafayette said in her most commanding voice.

Kora sat down at once, her back end coming down with a thump. She almost looked too heavy for a moment, like her front legs were trembling to hold her chest up. But then she evened out, and looked up at Lafayette with her tongue lolling once more.

"Yep. That's under your control," Lafayette said. "I'm sure you'll get smoother at it with practice. But it looks like it feels good. Does it feel good, Kora?"

"Lafayette!" Kora said.

Lafayette spent the rest of the second day going over the pages of that journal again. But as much as she thought she understood how all the parts fit together now, she didn't see anything else she could comfortably mess with. She didn't want to risk breaking Kora, after all.

When she woke on the morning of the third day, the idea of spending yet another day in camp really didn't appeal at all. Kora wasn't the only one who desperately wanted a walk.

So after a breakfast of rehydrated eggs and something that was probably meant to be sausage, Lafayette put her journal in her satchel with the positioning device and her canteen, and the two of them headed due north. To the ridge where they had first entered the jungle.

It was a short hike, only a couple of hours over mostly dry terrain. She had passed this way often enough that most of the walk was familiar territory, making it easy to avoid the few patches where there was mud.

The last bit of the way was up a path so steep it was almost more of a climb than a walk. Lafayette enjoyed the exercise, grasping outcroppings of rock when she could reach them to take some of the work off her straining leg muscles.

But Kora just floated up, touching down here and there to push off with one lazy swipe of a paw.

Lafayette had been worried that Kora would need to learn to control the hover disc's levels so she could stay down when she needed to. But Kora had mastered that and had moved on to controlling the levels in the other direction, apparently. She could make herself closer to weightless with a thought now.

And Lafayette had only wedged that pinhead a little closer to halfway in its notch. Such a small adjustment. But Kora was handling the change just fine.

For her part, Lafayette was entirely out of breath by the time she reached the top of the rocky ridge. She immediately flopped down on the first patch of level ground she reached and just stared up at the sky as she waited for the jabbing in her side to abate.

It was deep indigo, that sky, dotted with the sort of massive, puffy clouds that meant fair weather would persist for the rest of the day.

She had missed that sky.

"Lafayette," Kora said as she sprawled out on her belly close at Lafayette's side. She settled her nose on her paws and instantly fell into a deep sleep.

But as tired as her legs were from the climb, Lafayette felt no urge to nap. Instead, she sat up, digging her ration bar lunch out of her pack. She bit into it carefully, but also had her other hand cupped beneath it to catch the bits that would inevitably crumble away no matter how careful she was. That handful of bits was the result of every other mouthful when she ate one of these bars. She was used to it by now.

As she chewed, she looked out over the jungle spread out below her. It had seemed immensely huge when she had first seen it. But now that she'd spent ten days down in it, hiking from point to point, she had a different perspective on it. It was still huge, there was no denying that. And the greenness of it all was still unrelenting. It still wanted to be seen as a sea of liquid green, poured into a bowl of stone.

But she was pretty sure her eyes could pick out the divot in the tree cover where the campsite was.

She summoned up a mental map of all the places she had gone in the last ten days and tried to pinpoint them with her extended finger, scattered around the campsite and west and south of it.

She dropped her hand and wrapped her arms around her legs, resting her chin on her knees as she looked at the very center of the valley. When she had first seen this view, she had assumed that little rise in the treetops was because the trees were taller there.

But now she wasn't so sure. There was a sameness about the jungle trees that she had only noticed after days of walking among them. The plants that grew beneath the canopy were varied and numerous. But she was pretty sure that every tree down there was just a different example of the same kind of tree.

There was no reason for them to get suddenly taller in the center of things.

And there was definitely no reason for them to get two to three times taller, which was what it looked like she was seeing.

Somewhere in those trees, her father had placed the second beacon. Probably because it was a higher point of elevation.

But maybe there was more to it than that. Because that place, the center of the valley, was where he had told her he was going.

There had to be something there more than just really tall trees.

Lafayette got to her feet, stretched, then left Kora napping where she was to cross to the other side of the ridge. It wasn't far; when they had camped here on the trip in her father had had to cut down the perimeter fence to half its normal size because there wasn't enough room to put it up here.

But from the other side, Lafayette saw a whole other world. Her whole world, for most of her life. Sure, the grasslands she was looking down at now were wild. There weren't any other human beings for as far as her eye could see. But it was home.

Or had been.

She could see the road that led back to her village, off to the north and east.

But she could also see where a second road forked off of that road about halfway between her and the distant horizon. And that more northerly road led to a place she'd never been.

The capital.

Her parents had met there, when they were just a little older than Lafayette was now. They'd both been students of the historian Uche Okafo. For a time, anyway.

She had never been to the capital, but she had met Uche Okafo exactly twice. The first time had been when she was about six, and he had definitely made an impression. He had been the oldest man she had ever seen, with a face lined with heavily wrinkles and frizzy hair that had gone completely white, standing out starkly against skin that was darker even than her momma's.

But he'd also been the largest man she had ever seen. He had towered even taller than her father, and at six she hadn't even imagined that was possible. His shoulders were so wide that, if she could've gotten up the courage to try to hug him, she didn't think her arms would stretch far enough for her hands to reach around him.

He had spent several days that winter in her mother's little hut at the edge of the village. It had been quite crowded, as her father had been there too. But it had been a good kind of crowded, and Lafayette had basked in the attention of a rare adult outside of her two parents who wanted to admire her drawings or watch her turn cartwheels in the garden.

But at six, it hadn't ever occurred to her to wonder why that man had come to see her parents. Or what they were discussing together in whispers after they thought she had gone to sleep for the night.

Whatever it had been, he had gone back to the capital on the first day that dawned clear enough for traveling. And Lafayette hadn't seen him again.

Not until her mother's last days.

By the time he arrived, Lafayette had gotten used to the idea that no one was going to be able to help make her momma well again. She had been through all of her mother's journals, and she was certain if there was anything in there that her mother knew but was simply too sick to tell Lafayette what to do, she would've found it herself.

Still, a spark of hope had flared up inside her when she saw Uche Okafo standing in her doorway.

He must've seen that spark in her eyes, but he didn't say a word. He had just shaken his head, slowly and sadly. And Lafayette had nodded and led him inside to where her mother was resting.

If you could call it resting when she almost never woke up anymore.

Lafayette chewed at her lip, really wishing she could banish these dark thoughts away. The brighter green of the grasslands under the indigo sky, with the cool breeze blowing the sweaty hair back from her face, it should all really be enough to keep her from getting maudlin.

But she couldn't push these thoughts away. Not now. She needed to think them.

She needed to consider the offer that Uche had made to her before her momma died. The one she hadn't officially turned down.

After two days at her momma's bedside, Uche had told Lafayette that he couldn't stay any longer. He had to get back to the capital.

But would she like to go with him?

She hadn't said no. She had never said no.

But she hadn't said yes either.

How could she? Her momma, sick as she was, wasn't dead yet. How could Lafayette go?

To his credit, Uche had seemed to grasp this conundrum without her having to put it into words. He had just promised to get word to her father, and then, with one last pat to Kora's head, he had left.

But he had kept his promise. He had done the thing that Lafayette had no idea how to do on her own. He had gotten word to her father.

Of course, her father had gotten there too late. Her momma had been dead already by the time he reached their doorway.

But Uche had kept his promise.

And Lafayette was pretty sure his offer would still be open. If she could make it to the capital. If she could somehow find him in the city.

She had never seen a city. But from what she had heard, they were huge. Like, bigger than the jungle behind her.

And they were full of people. It would be easier to find one specific person in the jungle behind her than in a city, she feared.

If, if, if.

But still. It was an option.

And the man who had taught her parents everything was definitely not going to have a problem with Lafayette devoting her life to studying their journals, to writing her own with everything she could learn.

And that was something that was definitely not an option if she took the other road. If she went back to the village that was no longer her home.

She didn't have her mother's skills. She couldn't be their medicine woman. They would take her in. There was no question about that. They would keep her fed and clothed. They would give her a roof over her head and walls to keep out the wind.

But she knew what sort of work she'd be doing to earn all of that kindness. It was hard, backbreaking work. Work that would leave her no energy to study, even if she could do it in the dark of night when no one would know.

And she wouldn't be able to bring Kora with her. That had been very clear as she and Kora had followed her father out of the village. Kora, as she was now, was something they didn't understand, and they didn't *want* to understand.

No, there was really only one road to follow on the far side of this ridge.

But it wasn't time to follow it, anyway. She still had another day before her father was officially late.

And—a fact she had kept careful track of without quite admitting to herself why she was tracking it—she had enough supplies to last ten more days after that. Ten more days, and then if she wanted to reach the capital, the village, or anyplace at all before she ran out of food, she'd have to start walking.

She'd have to leave her father behind.

But today was not that day.

As if sensing a decision had been made, Kora woke from her nap with a shake, then stood up and trotted over to take her place at Lafayette's side.

The two of them headed back down into the jungle.

And in the morning, they would start a countdown of days for a second time. Only this time, it was just ten days. Ten days of waiting. And trying to keep hoping.

CHAPTER 7

Lafayette had assumed that if anything in the jungle got close enough to test out the perimeter fence, she would hear them coming first. The growly yowling would get closer, for one. But even if whatever made those noises decided to stalk silently up to the fence, surely she'd hear the sound of everything else getting quiet at their approach.

Because every night the cacophony of night birds calling to each other, of skittering little creatures moving from cover to cover in the thick undergrowth, of insects droning on and on for whatever reason insects droned, all of that was like a lullaby to her. She would climb into her sleeping bag, tuck Kora's warm body close to hers, and let her mind drift off to sleep on waves of those sounds.

She had been so sure that if that lullaby ever stopped, she'd be awake in a flash like a cranky baby whose mother had tried to stop singing.

But if those noises had stopped or even just diminished, she had slept on blissfully unaware.

Until the impossibly loud shriek of the alarms.

Somehow, they hadn't sounded so heart-stoppingly shrill in

daylight when her father had shown her the system the day they'd set up camp.

But in the dark of night, they definitely were. She felt her heart seize up in her chest and she actually got lightheaded in the split second before it started beating again.

Beating oh so fast.

Kora was growling, the hair on the back of her neck bristling the way it used to down her entire spine when she had gotten spooked by something back home in the village.

Lafayette rolled out of the sleeping bag and yanked on her boots without tying up the laces. Then she picked up the only weapon her father had left her with, a shock stick designed to herd farm animals into enclosures.

The farmers back home tried not to use them for any but the most foul-tempered of beasts, but Lafayette had seen how they worked once or twice. She knew it would be effective against all but the largest of creatures.

But she could only use it on one at a time. And she had to get so close to the target to jab it with the stick.

She really, really hoped she'd never have to try it out.

But she gripped it tightly all the same, for what comfort it gave her.

She and Kora burst out of the tent into the darkness of night. A light rain was falling, so softly it scarcely made a sound against the canvas of the tent roof. But with that rain came overcast skies, and Lafayette could barely make out any details by the dim red light emitting from the remaining embers in the banked down campfire. There were no stars overhead. There wasn't even an outline of the treetops. They blended perfectly with the darkness of the clouded sky above.

Lafayette turned in a slow circle, the shock stick held at the ready as she made a thorough search around the camp. The alarm was still blaring, but there was no sign of any movement inside the fence.

Only after she'd made a second careful circle did she finally lower the shock stick then head to the nearest fence post to quiet the alarm.

Now she could hear the jungle. It was like everything around her was angry at the intrusion of that noise and was caught for a moment in full volume trying to shout over it. But they quickly fell silent again, as if embarrassed at their display of ire.

Or afraid that whatever had set off the alarm would find them if they didn't quiet down.

The birds weren't calling to each other, and the little creatures weren't skittering that Lafayette could hear. The insects were droning, but in a subdued sort of way. If they were like the insects back home, that was as much due to the current falling rain as anything else.

And she could hear that now, the softest of pitter-patters on the tent behind her.

Lafayette had crouched down to disable the alarm, but she stood up now, the shock stick low at her side. Not that she thought it would interfere with her perceptions or anything. It was more like she just really had to focus on hearing anything else behind the rain and insect sounds.

She had to focus on seeing anything besides black on black in the world around her.

She thought there were some shadows moving, but distantly, behind at least three rows of trees.

Kora must have seen them too, because she started growling low in her throat, a warning to Lafayette more than a threat to whatever was out there.

"Come on, Kora," Lafayette said at last, not sure if she'd seen anything at all or only imagined it. Kora stopped growling at once and padded after her, back into the tent.

Not that Lafayette had any hopes of getting back to sleep. No, after slipping out of her boots she chose instead to sit down at her father's travel desk and dig through the journals it contained.

She found the section in one of them where he had worked out his designs for that perimeter fence. She had learned a few things studying the schematics for Kora's core, and she could recognize now the way her father used a certain set of symbols to represent the flow of power from one post to the next. It was the same with the pieces that came together to make Kora's core.

She had to dig through five more journals to find the same sort of notation in a schematic for how he had made changes to the way the shock stick worked. She had known it was different from what the farmers in the village had used, mostly that it ran longer with few recharges.

Now she could see that her father had achieved that by changing the power it discharged with each blow. He even had sketched up a handy comparison chart.

One poke of the shock stick would be enough to get a sheep in line, according to his chart. It would recharge between jabs, if only a little. He figured it maxed out at about fifteen jabs. But if she was trying to manhandle a cow, she'd need to adjust the setting on the side of the stick to discharge all of its juice at once. It would recharge, but that would take fifteen minutes, and it would still only be up to handling another sheep.

Lafayette chewed at her lip. She had no idea what had tested the fence. Was it bigger than a sheep?

Was it bigger than a cow?

She was pretty sure there had been a pack of them, whatever they were. If she had actually seen movement in the trees and not just imagined it, it had been more than one thing moving.

She was tempted to get a light and check out the ground just outside the fence, to see if anything had left any trace in the mud. But if there was one thing she was absolutely sure of, it was that light would attract unwanted attention.

And the fence was like the shock stick in a lot of crucial ways. There was a limit to how much it could discharge at a time. If a bunch of animals tried to get through all at once, some of them were bound to succeed.

But she really hated the fact that she had no idea what she was up against.

She put on her boots and, careful to not wake Kora, she slipped back out into the rainy night. She went back to the post of the perimeter fence and checked its settings.

It was, indeed, still working to recharge whatever it had lost when the alarm had gone off before.

Something had taken a jolt. And then, since she could see no sign of anything anywhere, whatever it was must've been okay enough to run away again.

She didn't like the way that made her feel at all.

Worse, the alarm had gone off more than an hour before. And yet the fence wasn't back up to full strength yet.

Lafayette tried peering into the darkness again, but it was all just as inscrutable as it had been before. She could see flickering dots—the glowing insects—but only far off in the distance, and only in glimpses when no trees were standing between them and her.

She went back into the tent. Kora woke up and gave her an accusatory look for going outside without her companion, but when she saw Lafayette taking her boots off again, she settled back into sleep.

Lafayette envied her ability to do that. She was exhausted, but she knew sleep was never going to happen for her. Not until after daybreak, when she could search for clues.

Maybe not even then.

She had only ticked down two more days in the second ten-day countdown. There was still enough food for her to wait eight days more.

But now she had a different countdown to worry about.

Maybe whatever those creatures were, they'd only gotten bold because it was such a dark, rainy night. If the next eight nights were clear, starry skies again, they might stay away.

But if they didn't, if they'd only been testing the fence...

If they were intelligent enough to learn what Lafayette now knew about its limitations…

If they decided to come back...

Lafayette's mind didn't dare finish any of those thoughts. But it couldn't refrain from starting them either. The fragments just kept running in a loop over and over until the blackness of night became the gray of a post-rain dawn.

She wasn't entirely surprised to find no trace in the mud around the camp. The rain had been barely more than a drizzle, but it had left a watery layer on the top of the mud that barely hinted at indentations in its surface here or there. Nothing definitive enough to be a footprint.

She still didn't know their size, or have any clue how to guess their number.

But when the first light of dawn finally reached down through the canopy of trees to light up her campsite, she had already decided it didn't matter.

It wasn't safe to stay where she was. Not anymore.

She needed to get out of the jungle. To higher ground. Ground where she could see more than an arm's length away from her face. Where she could see danger coming.

It took Lafayette a lot longer to pack up the camp than it had for her father and her to set it up days before. Although she had left as much as she could inside the travel crates, she still had to haul all those crates onto the hover cart all by herself.

Not that she didn't give a thought or two to whether Kora could be modified to carry things on her back. But Lafayette would just have to load and unload the dog as well. That really wouldn't save her any time.

And the tent turned out to be more of a mystery than she had expected. She had thought she'd paid good attention when her father had shown her how to set it up, but apparently not. Or maybe just reversing all those steps wasn't the right way to get it back down again. In the end, she didn't quite get it all collapsed, but that was okay. It was still pretty wet from the night before, and draping its half-collapsed form over the top of everything else on the hover cart was probably the better plan anyway.

Or so she told herself.

She wished there was a way to ride the hovering cart back to the northern ridge, but alas the cart needed a hand to guide it or it didn't know which way to move. So once more she was trudging through the mud, but fresh mud this time. Mud that clung with extra tenacity to her boots.

It was like the jungle didn't want to let her go.

Kora floated as little as she could manage out of some sort of doggy solidarity. Lafayette appreciated the gesture, even if she was too tired to tell Kora that she was a good dog.

She was so exhausted. Moving the entire camp herself would've been a lot of work even if she hadn't been awake all night the night before.

Getting the cart up the steep path up to the ridge turned out to be easier than she feared, but only because the way her father had built it kept it level without regard to the slope of the ground beneath it. Nothing slid off the surface no matter how steep the path got.

It was still exhausting climbing to the ridge, but adding a few little pushes to keep the cart hovering forward didn't add to it too much.

But it was late in the afternoon by the time they reached the narrow plateau. Lafayette scrambled to set up the perimeter fence first, before darkness could catch her unprepared. She tested the system, then she tested it again.

She really wished she could test it for real, to know it was really functioning and not just telling her so on its settings panel. But she didn't want to ask Kora to do something like that, and if she did it to herself she'd just as likely be left lying completely unconscious outside of the fence as inside. And that would be really bad.

Plus, it would really upset Kora.

So she had to trust the panel wasn't lying to her.

She also had to set up the rest of the camp. But luckily the tent, the most important part, was already halfway there.

Lafayette couldn't remember ever being as tired as she was in that moment. But if she wanted to rest, she had to work more first.

So she set to it.

CHAPTER 8

The night was clear, and with no trees overhead, the stars just felt that much brighter. Like they were closer, so close Lafayette could reach up and touch them.

She was tempted to sleep outside the tent so she could watch for anything that might try climbing up the slope to her camp, but the ridge was far too windy for that. So once again, she slipped into her sleeping bag and cuddled Kora close.

"Lafayette," Kora said in a sleepy murmur, like she was already half in a dream.

Lafayette hoped it was a good one.

There were no birds up on this ridge, or at least none that called to each other after dark. There were a few of the droning insects, but their sounds were nearly always drowned out by the sound of the wind flapping the sides of the tent and whistling through the rocky promontory just west of where Lafayette had set up the camp.

The beacon that marked the north of the valley was on top of that promontory, she knew.

And somewhere in that clump of what appeared to be the tallest trees was the other beacon.

And her father.

Lafayette marked off five more uneventful days up on top of the ridge. Nothing tested her fence again. It was just her and Kora and the constant mournful whistling of the wind.

But with only two days of waiting around rations left before she'd have to start digging into what they'd need for the walk back to civilization, Lafayette decided not to wait any longer.

She had to go find her father. It might take more than a day to find him.

But really, the fact of the matter was that she simply couldn't sit and wait any longer.

She packed the last of the waiting around rations in her satchel, along with as much water as she could carry and her own journal. She tucked the positioning disc into the side pocket where she could reach it easily. She wouldn't have to hunt for a signal or crosscheck its sigils with the map in her journal this time. All she had to do was make sure the direction she was walking was still the one that made the green light glow. If it looked dim, she would just have to nudge her heading a little more directly in its path. And if it stopped glowing, she'd know she'd gone too far.

She just needed to follow a straight line until she got to the beacon. Then she'd start hunting for signs of her father.

For the path down the ridge to the edge of the jungle, that plan worked exactly as she had intended. She kept walking in a straight line towards that point in the center of the valley.

But things changed the minute she was back inside the canopy of trees. She could no longer see the point she was heading towards in front of her. The treetops were too dense for that.

Even following the heading on her positioning disc didn't work out as well as she had thought. There was simply too much in her way. She was constantly skirting around mud patches that were too wide and too thick to wade through. Or making her way around fallen trees that didn't look stable enough to attempt to climb over. Or avoiding thickets of plants she already knew were too covered in sharp thorns for her to push her way through without getting covered in scrapes that were bound to get infected.

Worse, she couldn't always just get back on the true path after making one of these detours. There was always something else that got in the way. And some of the detours were really backtracks, and that was the most frustrating of all.

She stopped for lunch on the trunk of a smaller fallen tree, one she was sure wasn't going to shift and roll under her weight. She filled the water bowl for Kora, but saved her own water for after she'd eaten her ration bar, when she'd really want it to clear the taste out of her mouth and rinse the last of the stickiness off of her teeth.

She didn't know how far she'd come, but she had a sinking feeling it wasn't anywhere near as far as she should've.

And lunchtime was really too late in the day to realize she had made no plan for what she would do when it got dark if she hadn't found her father yet.

He had been doing something, surely. He had been on his own outside of the camp for so many nights, he must have some plan for how to keep safe.

But he hadn't shared it with her. And she had no clue how to start.

"Lafayette?" Kora said.

"Right," Lafayette said, and pushed herself back to her feet to resume the hike. At least after so many days just sitting around the campsite waiting, she was feeling fresh. She had a lot more walking in her.

But she didn't like the feeling that a lot more walking was just what was going to be required.

Or the feeling like the jungle around her was getting darker in a way that had nothing to do with the hour of the day. It was barely past noon. Intuitively, she knew the sun was high in the sky somewhere just over her head.

But she couldn't feel it. She couldn't see its light or feel its warmth. The canopy that stretched out over her head was too dense for that. The trees reached their branches out far and wide, entangling them with all the other branches from all the other trees. No ray of sunshine stood any chance of penetrating that.

But something lived up there. She could hear it, rustling through the leaves as it ran, scratching at the bark with its talons or nails or whatever.

Not that she ever saw anything. It was simply too dark. Everything overhead was a deep, dark green that on some level she still saw as rather pretty. It was so much more lush than the greens of the fields at home. They looked watered-out by comparison.

As the afternoon wore on, she gained a new worry. Shouldn't the land be getting hillier here? It did to the south from the campsite. She was a bit east of that area, but shouldn't it still be hilly here?

Or had she been wrong about the height of the trees? Was there really a stand of gigantically immense trees in the heart of the valley?

If only she could see through the canopy, even just a glimpse. She would feel better if she knew she was getting closer.

Or better yet, what it was she was getting closer *to*.

But mostly her eyes had to be down, down on her feet as she chose the driest path through the ever-wider expanses of foul-smelling mud. The undergrowth was sparser here, where the canopy was so dense. But the mud was far, far fouler. It had a sickly green slickness to it, a sheen she really didn't want to get on her skin.

But it wasn't like she could help it. That mud topped out her boots from time to time. Her socks were a sodden mess. Her feet were going to be horrific when she finally sat down to take everything off them and see.

"Lafayette?" Kora said. She had that plaintive tone to her voice again. This place was making her nervous as much as it was Lafayette.

"We're on the right path," Lafayette assured her as she reached out for a branch to pull herself out of the latest mud patch on to higher, drier ground.

Kora was gliding on her hover disc openly now. She had given up the idea of joining Lafayette in getting really muddy at some point just past lunchtime. Not that Lafayette minded. She just wished she could do the same.

The smell of the mud was following her now, there was so much of it caked all the way up to her knees. She smelled like she'd been wading in dead things. Probably because she had.

But when she had made sure to anchor both her feet before taking the disc out to check, she had been correct. They were still heading towards the beacon. They were going the right way.

There was nothing more to be done but to continue on.

But the next lake of mud had a new element to it: bugs. Great clouds of insects that were individually too small for Lafayette to really see. She couldn't even catch one, they were so small and so fast. But they hovered around her sweaty face and neck in a stinging cloud. She could feel them sinking into the slick of her perspiration, wiggling around there before biting her with sharp needle-like teeth. Or whatever it was that insects bit with.

They were too small to slap effectively, but she could rub them away by scrubbing at her skin with her hand.

Not that it mattered. They came back just as quickly as her sweat did.

And the mud she had gotten on her hands despite her best efforts not to touch anything got all over her face and neck, making the dead thing smell that much stronger in her nostrils.

It didn't deter the little bugs at all.

"Lafayette," Kora said in a complaining tone. Lafayette looked down to see dozens of the little things all over the corners of Kora's eyes. The dog shook her head, scattering them into an angry cloud around her head. But they just settled back into place the minute the motion stopped.

"We've got to get to the other side, I think," Lafayette said. "Hover on up ahead. I'll catch up."

"Lafayette," Kora said. Lafayette couldn't parse that tone at all, but it must have been a refusal of her suggestion, because Kora stayed just where she was, hovering by Lafayette's side.

They reached the far side of the mud lake, but the bugs clung with them. Like they were curious where the two of them were heading. Lafayette planted her feet and checked their heading, made a minuscule adjustment, then put the disc away and hiked on. Kora followed without a word.

And the world just kept getting darker. Lafayette spared as many glances up as she could, desperate for any sign of the trees getting taller or the terrain getting hillier. But everything carried on as before. The only change was that growing darkness.

Only this time, it really did mean the sun was gone. It was setting somewhere unseen off to the west.

"Lafayette?" Kora said, sounding truly miserable now.

"It's all right," Lafayette said as she dug through her satchel. She had brought a single light with her. It wouldn't illuminate much, but hopefully that meant it wouldn't attract much either. She held it low, close to the ground. It would be enough to make out the details of the mud in front of her. It would be enough to keep her out of sinkholes.

She hoped.

"We'll get there soon," she told the dog, although she didn't quite believe it herself. "We just have to."

They walked on for only a few more minutes before reaching the densest tangle of vines she had yet seen. They were living versions of the vines she had twisted into rope days before, thick and climbable.

Not that there was any point in climbing them. They'd only take her up into the trees. And as much as she'd not yet attempted such a thing, she knew there would be no safety there.

She had heard enough sounds up there to deduce that well enough.

She was just about to turn to find a way around this latest obstruction when something caught the corner of her eye. A brief gleam through the leaves that adorned the sides of the thick vines.

A metallic gleam.

"Lafayette?" Kora asked as Lafayette turned back to look more closely.

"There's something in here," Lafayette told her as she set the light on the ground to use both hands to part the leaves. "Maybe another artifact. Or maybe something my father dropped if he came this way."

Either would be good. But if she was being honest, at that point she really hoped for the latter.

But whatever was in there was too large to be an artifact, and it was definitely too large to be something her father dropped.

Her fingers brushed against an entire surface of metal, cold and flat beyond the vines. She pressed her palm flat against it. Then she reached up and down, left to right, as far as she could. The vines tightened around her arm, cutting down her range of motion, but not too much for her to know that whatever was on the other side was huge.

Bigger than the side of her tent, anyway.

But the vines were too dense for her to see more than a glimpse of it, especially by the light of a solitary lamp.

She should've brought some sort of cutting tool, but perhaps it was just as well. The idea of standing here sawing away at things as the last of the light of day died away really creeped her out. She'd be too engrossed to notice anything that crept up behind her.

"Lafayette," Kora said again, her voice low. Almost as if she had had the same thought.

But when Lafayette pulled her arm back out of the vines, she realized the dog wasn't looking at her.

She was looking at the ground below the lamp.

Lafayette squatted to look, too. The ground here was not so much dry as mossy. Better than mud for walking, that was for sure.

But not the best for finding and identifying footprints.

Still, her heart started to beat faster as she realized that there *was* something there. Kora had found something.

It was only the suggestion of an outline, to be sure, but still. She just knew she wasn't imagining it.

There was the clear outline of a boot print, smashing down the delicate fronds of the moss. And it wasn't her boot print. For one, her feet were still where she had planted them. She hadn't stepped that far to her right, even when she'd been trying to find the limits of whatever it was on the far side of the vines.

But, more importantly, that print had come from a boot easily twice the size of hers.

A boot like her father had.

She had found him. Or, she'd almost found him. But she'd find him for real soon enough. It had taken all day, but she'd done it.

"Come on, Kora," Lafayette said, creeping forward in a low, stooping walk as she scanned the ground ahead for another boot print.

And found it. Then another. And another.

"Lafayette," Kora said, sounding relieved.

Lafayette felt bad she'd made the dog so nervous, but it was all right now.

They'd be with her father soon, and everything would be just fine.

CHAPTER 9

The tracks left by her father's boots were really easy to follow for the first five minutes. They ran parallel to the metallic wall that Lafayette could still catch occasional glimpses of through the dense mat of vines that otherwise completely covered it.

But then, without any warning or any sign of why, they just stopped.

Lafayette backtracked a few steps, crouching low to play the light over the thick, muddy ground. But the last two footprints she had seen before were still the only ones she could see now. One right step, then one left step, and then… what?

Had he hovered up into the air like Kora on her belly disc?

Lafayette was almost smiling at this image when she heard a low growl directly overhead.

Overhead, and so very close.

"Lafayette?" Kora said in whimper.

Lafayette had frozen in her crouched position, not daring to move the light or even to lift her head to look up. Her heart was beating so fast, and yet her blood felt icy cold as it coursed through her veins.

Then she heard another growl, a slightly different growl from a position a little more to her left.

And then a third, from a little to her right.

Three of those things were close to her, close enough to touch her, she was sure. But they were all directly overhead.

And exactly at the position where her father had stopped walking.

She had a different image in her mind now. Not an amusing one of a suddenly levitating version of her father. No, this image was far bloodier.

But there was no blood on the ground. She still didn't dare move the light or her head to be sure, but she had been looking everywhere for boot prints. If there had been sprays of blood over the surface of the ground, she would've seen it. Even in the bluish light from the lamp, she would've seen something.

Which didn't rule out him being hauled up into the treetops and carried away, to be torn to pieces somewhere else.

"Lafayette?" Kora said again. Lafayette glanced over and saw the dog was looking up. Kora could see what was stalking them.

Then Lafayette heard the sound of something moving over her head, jumping from one branch to land with a rustle and a low growl on another. Then the other two creatures shifted position as well. As if they were performing some sort of dance for her. They weren't leaving, but they also weren't advancing or pouncing. They were just circling.

Lafayette was still frozen in place, gazing intently at her father's last boot print. As if, if she could focus enough on one thing, she could make the rest of the world just go away.

But there was something different about that boot print. Most of them were deeper at the ball of the foot, but this one was deeper right at the toe. The change was pretty pronounced. But what did it mean?

The creatures above kept up almost a continuous low growl. But they didn't move. She could feel all their eyes boring into her, but they weren't moving yet.

Lafayette gripped the lamp's handle so tightly her fingers were digging into her own flesh. But somehow she found the will to lift it just a little higher. Then she lifted her head, just a little. Just enough to look up. Not at the things that were stalking her—she wasn't *that* brave —but at the wall of vines in front of her.

Did it look like her father had climbed those vines? She could see broken stems of leaves here and there, and even an entire thinner vine that had snapped, then collapsed to the ground. It looked pretty wilted now, like it had broken days ago.

Had he jumped and climbed? Was there a place of safety up there in the darkness? Or had this just been where he had chosen to scramble over the wall?

Lafayette raised the lamp a little higher with one trembling hand, then took a step forward. She was still crouched low to the ground, not looking up. But when the low growl overhead carried on unchanged, she risked a second step. Then a third, and a fourth.

And now she was close enough to touch the vines. But she couldn't climb with the lamp in her hand.

"Kora," Lafayette said, flinching at the way her voice squeaked that one word out.

"Lafayette," Kora said. She had followed Lafayette up to the vines, but was keeping an eye on whatever was in the trees above them.

"I need to climb from here. Can you hover up after me?"

"Lafayette," Kora said.

Lafayette could only hope that meant yes.

She had no way of hanging the lamp off her clothes or the outside of her satchel, so she had no choice but to stow it away. She left the top flap of her satchel open, but the light that managed to escape that way was dim, and pretty much blocked by the motion of her arms.

But there wasn't anything she wanted to see, anyway. She'd prefer not knowing what she was really hoping was going to just watch her go on by. And she didn't need to see much to climb the vines. Their matted mass was so thick, she only had to reach out to find any number of good handholds.

She was only about a meter or two off the ground when she heard all those watching creatures moving at once.

There were so many more than three of them. The others had just been silent until now.

Now, they were all yowling like the shrillest of screams. And they were crashing through the trees all around her, closing in on the three who had been keeping watch.

Lafayette felt a surge of adrenaline that demanded that she scramble up the vine-covered wall with all due speed.

But she couldn't. Not until she had eyes on Kora. She had to know Kora was following her. She couldn't bear leaving Kora behind.

Then she really would be alone.

Her heart sank when she saw Kora was still standing on the ground below. But she had turned to put her back end towards the wall, not like she was going to leave, but like she was covering Lafayette while she climbed.

Then, as Lafayette watched, Kora threw back her head and howled. It started as her usual doggy howl—not that Kora had ever howled much, or had ever had reason to when living in the village—but then built into something strange and horrific.

Lafayette couldn't describe it, even to herself as she was hearing it. It was like it kept building and building, getting shriller and shriller. And then she couldn't hear it at all. But she could still feel it, in her bones. Kora was still howling, Lafayette knew it. She just couldn't hear it with her human ears.

Then the growls of the creatures around them turned to yowls of pain. Lafayette's ears were still ringing from the last high-pitched bit of howling she had heard, but she could hear the sounds of things fleeing through the trees. The world was muffled, but she knew she was right. She could see branches breaking and falling to the ground, raining down around Kora who still stood stock still with her head thrown back, mouth open as that inaudible howl droned on.

Then something bumped Lafayette's shoulder. She yelped, clinging tighter to the vines in her hands. But the thing that had bumped her was too much in a hurry to get away to bother with her. She got a glimpse of a shape like a cat, only a cat twice the size of Kora, almost as large as one of the sheep back in the village.

Then the thing gave up trying to scramble up the vines as Lafayette had been doing. It sprang away from the wall, stretching its legs wide. Even its paws spread wide, each of its toes unfurled. They were tipped with nails like talons that glinted evilly in the escaped light from Lafayette's satchel.

The thing had webbed toes. No cat Lafayette had ever seen had had webbed toes. Of course, no cat Lafayette had ever seen had been the size of a sheep, either.

Then the legs snapped out to their maximum extension, and Lafayette saw little membranes of skin that stretched from forelimb to back limb. The membranes filled like a sheet hung to dry in the wind, billowing and catching the air.

The thing didn't exactly fly, and it didn't hover like Kora. But it did glide from a spot just above Lafayette's head to a branch that hung low to the ground on the far side of Kora.

It hit that branch with all four paws, and the membranes whisked back out of sight. In a flash, it had scrabbled away, disappearing into the darkness.

"Lafayette," Kora said, and Lafayette realized the dog had finally started to hover, pausing at her eye level as it spoke at her in a chastising voice.

"I'm climbing," Lafayette said, and turned her attention back to the task.

Those things had run away, but whatever Kora had done had only spooked them. It hadn't really hurt them.

They would be back. And they would be angry.

Lafayette had no clear idea of how long she climbed or how high. The adrenaline rushing through her system was making every flash of a second feel like an eternity, but the succession of seconds went by all in a rush. It was very confusing.

And it was starting to make her hands shake.

She was still climbing, hand after hand, foot after foot, when she heard the sounds of growling drawing closer around her once more.

Yes, they definitely sounded like they'd come back angry.

They'd also come back with even more friends.

"Lafayette," Kora said.

"I'm hurrying, I'm hurrying," Lafayette said through labored breaths. She gritted her teeth, but made every effort to climb faster.

Just how tall was this wall?

She remembered the height of the treetops as she'd seen them from the ridge to the north. This wall could very well be taller than she could climb without a rest.

And with nothing but vines within reach, she had no way of getting that rest. She would climb until she couldn't, and then she would fall.

It was a long way down. She didn't know how long exactly, but she had no illusions about it being a fall she could survive.

Her top hand reached for the next vine but closed over nothingness. It was a jerking feeling, like missing a step on a staircase. Her feet and her other hand were all securely positioned in the mat of vines, so she was in no danger, but that jerking feeling was very different hundreds of meters up in the sky than it was at the bottom of a staircase.

"Lafayette!" Kora said. Not in worry—Lafayette wasn't sure if she had even noticed what had just happened with Lafayette's hand—but in what sounded like excitement.

Lafayette reached her hand up again, but this time instead of grasping for a vine, she spread her fingers wide, feeling around the open space.

She felt a metal edge. The wall she had been climbing had gone from vertical to horizontal. Looking up, she could see more vines over her head, so she wasn't at the top of the wall. But she had definitely reached a place where she could rest.

If it was large enough to sit in, that was.

She felt a smooth groove in the surface of the metal, deep enough for her to dig her fingers into and pull her body weight up with. She gripped it, brought her other hand up beside it, then scrambled over the edge.

And found herself in a space about the size of a doorway. Not the door into her mother's hut, more the size of the larger doors that led into the village meeting hall.

Anyway, it was more than large enough for Lafayette to rest. She crawled a bit away from the open ledge, keeping her back to what she thought of as the doorframe, and watched as Kora hovered up to sit across from her. Kora went back to the edge to look down in worry, but Lafayette just drew up her knees and rested her forehead on them.

Her arms were shaking. Her legs were shaking. Her whole body was shaking. But the adrenaline was fading, and without it, she was suddenly tired.

Tired, and oh so very cold.

"Lafayette," Kora said warningly.

"Can they climb this high?" Lafayette asked, then lifted her head to look out the opening.

There were indeed many trees that grew all around her little nook. The branches she could make out through the darkness looked sturdy enough to hold her weight, let alone the weight of one of those cat things. She didn't think she could jump across to even the nearest of those branches.

But those cat things, with their gliding wings, could almost certainly make the leap.

"I don't think we're safe here," Lafayette said, and forced herself to her feet. She didn't like how much she had to use the wall behind her for support just to get up. The climb had taken everything out of her. But what if the cats closed in for a fight? Would Kora's howl drive them back a second time?

Lafayette reached into her satchel for her light and held it up to see how deep the nook went.

Not very, only about a meter deep.

But the inside wall of the nook looked like a door. Not like any door she had ever seen, being all smooth, featureless metal. But it was covering what wanted to be an opening in front of her. It was, functionally, a door.

Lafayette frowned as something caught her eye, some blemish on that smooth metal surface. She was just leaning in, her fingers tracing a series of gouges at the edge of the door that definitely weren't from animal claws, when there was a thump of weight landing between her and Kora.

Then a yowl that echoed painfully, bouncing shrilly off all those metallic walls.

But not to the left of where Lafayette was touching the door.

Kora snarled and lunged at the cat thing that stood between her and Lafayette. The cat crouched low but only growled back. The cat's eyes never left Kora's, but for a moment the two animals were in a standoff of sorts.

That wouldn't last long.

But even as she had that thought, Lafayette realized the gouges she was still touching had come from some other metal tool scarring this metal door. Like someone had pried open this door.

Someone like her father?

To her left, where the cat's yowl hadn't echoed, there was an opening. But it was narrow. Almost too narrow.

But not quite. Lafayette was pretty sure if she turned sideways and sucked in her breath, she could squirm through.

Before she could test her theory, the cat suddenly lunged, not at Kora but at her. Lafayette yelped in alarm, scrambling back into the deepest corner of the nook.

But she also dropped her light. It bounced on the metal lip of the alcove with an ominous crunch. Then it rolled over the edge and out of sight. If it made any sound hitting the muddy jungle floor far below, there was too much noise in that alcove for Lafayette to hear it.

The cat was yowling, but it wasn't pouncing on Lafayette. Lafayette lowered her arms and realized that Kora was the reason the cat wasn't tearing her apart right that second. The dog had sunk her teeth deep into the cat's hindquarters. The cat twisted to hiss at Kora, but didn't get an opportunity to do more. Not before Kora just tossed her head, throwing the hissing cat out into the black of night.

The cat flew from Kora's jaws like it weighed no more than a sack of feathers. Was Kora just that strong, or was the cat's gliding body just that light?

Lafayette heard the cat's body impact a branch, and then another. But the third time it hit, it sounded like it caught hold. There was a rustle of leaves as it scrambled up to the relative safety of the crook, closer to the trunk. Then it went still.

But there were others, Lafayette knew.

"Kora, come on. In here," Lafayette said, pushing the dog through the crack between door and door frame.

"Lafayette!" Kora said, clearly upset at being pushed through first.

But Lafayette didn't respond to the dog. She just swung her satchel in after Kora, then squeezed through herself.

Her foot sent something metallic skittering across the floor. Probably the tool that had forced the door open. But she didn't spend a thought on it. This side of the door had a handle of sorts. It was large, like the rung of a ladder, but stood vertically at the edge of the door.

Lafayette moved to put that handle between her and the opening, then leaned in with all her might. At first, the door didn't want to move.

Then she heard the sound of another cat landing in the nook, then another. And she dug deeper and found more might to put to work shoving the door closed.

The door shrieked in protest, but it moved. Lafayette was yelling too as she finally got it going, centimeter by centimeter, closing the gap between her and Kora and the jungle outside.

One of the cats swiped at her ankle with a widely stretched paw, leaving four long bloody cuts through her thick sock and into her flesh. But the pain only gave her the last burst of strength she needed to get the door closed.

The cat withdrew its paw just in time. As Lafayette sagged against the door handle, she could hear it on the other side, screaming in frustration.

"Lafayette?" Kora said, her voice coming out of what was to Lafayette's eyes total darkness.

"I'm okay," Lafayette said. "I just need a minute."

She knew she should clean those cuts. And she could really use a drink of water.

But rather than do either of those things, her head rolled back against the cold metal of the door behind her, and her eyes slid shut against that darkness.

She only needed a minute. That was her last thought.

She vaguely felt Kora's tongue worrying at the wound on her leg. But then sleep took her, and she knew no more.

CHAPTER 10

Lafayette woke up to find herself curled up on her side, Kora tucked in close against her stomach. That position was completely normal. But the lack of the warmth of her sleeping bag was not.

And the cold, smooth metal under her was definitely not normal.

"Lafayette," Kora said, as if she had been waiting forever for Lafayette to wake up. Which, maybe she had. Because what had been pitch blackness before was now patches of darker and lighter gray.

Lafayette sat up, then looked at the door behind her. She had pushed it closed enough to keep the cat things out, but she hadn't shoved it all the way flush. There was a little gap, just enough to let in a single shaft of light.

But it was more light than Lafayette was used to seeing through the filtering of the jungle treetops. It didn't penetrate deeply into the darkness on the far side of the door, but it filled that gap in the doorway with warm, yellow light.

Lafayette got up and went over to the handle, leaning her weight into it in the opposite direction as the night before. It complained a little, but moved ever so slightly more easily than it had the first time.

When there was enough space for her to slip through, she stopped pushing and went outside.

Many cats had been here the night before. Not that she had heard them; she had slept more soundly than she had since leaving the village weeks before. But they had left signs of their presence.

Smelly signs.

Lafayette waved a hand under her nose, but resisted the urge to retreat back to the other side of the door. As intense as that ammonia smell was, the cats were all gone now. And the warmth of the sun felt glorious.

There were still tree branches spread out overhead, but not as many. And she could see the sky through the canopy in a lot of spots. A particularly large gap between two trees was allowing the rising sun to fill the nook, although she could tell that wouldn't last long.

But everything around where she was standing was more in shadow. Lafayette grabbed onto more vines and pulled herself out of the metallic nook, swinging to the left side then climbing a few meters. Then there was another lip she could pull herself over, although this lip seemed to be metallic at its core, but covered with about half a meter of crumbling earth, then another half a meter of decaying leaves and fallen vines from trees that towered over her.

While what she had climbed the night before was a sheer vertical drop to the jungle floor below, this side was more like a very steep hill. It wouldn't be an easy climb, especially with its top layer being slimy, decaying plant matter with no trustworthy handholds and who knew how stable your footing would be.

But it *was* like a hillside in that there were trees growing on it. They looked quite desperate, their roots barely covered by the loam, knotty, twisted bits of wood grasping for support that looked precarious at best.

But they were tall, as tall as the trees further below.

So that answered *that* question.

Lafayette crept back down to the nook, suddenly far more nervous about relying on the vines to hold her weight now that she'd seen how little was holding them anchored. She took a few deep breaths once she was back to standing on both feet. She edged forward, as close to the edge as she dared, then looked down. Her stomach turned over with a sickening flop at the sight below her.

The ground was so far down she couldn't even see it. There were too many waving branches of tree growth between her and that mud.

"Lafayette?" Kora said as she strode more bravely to the very edge and leaned over to see what Lafayette was looking at.

"I was just thinking about climbing down to see how broken that light is, but I think it's hopeless," Lafayette said with a sigh. She had heard the crunch when it had fallen from her hand to the metal floor. If that hadn't broken it badly, the second fall to the ground below certainly had.

Kora just kept looking down. Lafayette could see the dog's nose wrinkling again and again as she tested the air. Although how she could smell anything past the reek of urine in the nook was beyond Lafayette.

"I'm going to clean up those scratches," Lafayette said as she ducked back in through the doorway. Better late than never, she hoped.

She had only been outside for a moment, but her eyes were already sun-dazzled. She groped around for her satchel, then dug through it by touch until she found her first aid kit.

The wound was pretty clean already, thanks to Kora's fastidious licking. Lafayette smeared it liberally with one of her mother's antibiotic concoctions. Then she wrapped her entire ankle in a clean white bandage, around and around until every bit of the wound was covered.

That cat thing had cut her up pretty good with one blind strike. Lafayette was very glad she had gotten through the doorway before it could do more. Or before the others had joined it to overwhelm her with sheer numbers.

She was just shuddering at the image of being at the bottom of a pile of those angry, hissing things when Kora came back through the doorway with her head held high, like she was quite proud of herself. Then she dropped something in Lafayette's lap just as she was pinning down the end of the bandage to keep it from unwinding when she moved.

"What's this?" Lafayette asked, but the minute her fingers touched it, she knew what it was.

It was the light she had dropped the night before. Kora must have deployed her hover disc again. She had gone down and fetched it.

"Kora, that's the most doggy thing I've seen you do in ages," Lafayette said, scratching all around Kora's ears. Kora said nothing, but the happy thump of her long red tail on the ground behind her said enough.

The light in Lafayette's hands was inert, dark. But her fingertips found the switch for the power. It was currently on the off setting. It must've gotten bumped in the fall.

Lafayette slid the switch over, and the light in her hands mustered up a faint purple glow. But it only lasted for a second at that intensity before fading ever so slowly back to inert darkness.

"Lafayette?" Kora said, sounding disappointed.

"No, this is good," Lafayette assured her. "It's not broken. It just needs a charge."

Of course, the only thing she had to charge it with was back at the camp on the north ridge. With her sleeping bag. And most of the rest of the food.

She had four ration bars in her satchel, as well as Kora's food paste. But she didn't have much water left.

She gave Kora the portion of paste she should've had the night before, and she licked it up with her usual gusto. Lafayette tried to savor her ration bar, but even as hungry as she was after missing dinner the night before, she couldn't pretend she enjoyed the experience. It seemed to cling to her teeth with extra alacrity, as if it knew she didn't have enough water to properly wash it all down.

If her stomach hadn't been an angry, empty knot, she would've skipped it entirely. But she knew she needed the calories. She had done a lot of climbing the day before.

And looking at the way the floor in front of her sloped away from where she huddled by the door, it was a good bet she was going to have even more climbing to do today.

As she slowly chewed her bar, she examined a ridge in the floor only about a meter inside the doorway. It didn't look like it was deliberate. The metal had a puffy, scarred kind of look. She didn't have a huge amount of experience with metal. The homes in her village were largely built of local materials. Like what stones could be found while tilling the fields. The rare bits of wood scavenged years ago. But mainly the abundant mud, and grass woven into mats and then covered with that mud.

Metal was too precious to build with. It needed to be used in tools.

But as far as she could tell from what she'd seen the night before and what she was looking at now, she was in the most immense structure she had ever been inside. And the whole thing looked like it was made of metal.

She didn't understand that at all. She couldn't wrap her mind around it.

She had heard stories about the buildings in the capital, sure. How they were so tall they looked like they were going to pierce the sky. How their halls were so large that the people of a hundred villages at once could meet inside one.

But those buildings had all been built from stone. At least, from what she had heard or read about the city.

And none of them had been the size of what she was standing in now.

Not that what she could see in front of her was all that impressive, actually. It appeared to be just a normal hallway. She could see doorways along its length, some open although the rooms beyond were in darkness, some closed with doors that were, of course, also made of metal.

No, the only thing really exceptional about it was that it rose up before her at a steep angle, as steep as the path from the jungle up to the north ridge. And it was twisted. The twist was most pronounced where she was at the moment, just at that seam in the metal that felt like a scar. Like she was touching the last vestiges of a terrible wound in the structure itself.

She couldn't see far. But something about the quality of the air, the way the few sounds she and Kora were making were swallowed up by that air, gave her a sense like that hallway just kept rising up forever.

Well, she knew that wasn't true. She had seen from the north ridge that it didn't go up forever. It didn't even go up higher than the tree-tops she had just been looking at a moment before.

But maybe it didn't have to keep going up to keep going forever. Maybe it dove down at some point.

She had seen how far down some of the artifacts she had found had gone into the earth when she had collected them. A few of the larger ones had been more underground than above. Some had barely been visible on the surface at all, but had ended up far larger than that first glimpse had led her to expect.

The same could be true of this structure. Especially if it had fallen from the sky with the same force as had driven those objects deep into the ground at the bottom of the craters.

Which Lafayette was beginning to think it had. Really, the jungle looked like it sat inside the confines of a bowl because it did. Only that bowl should more properly be called a crater, she supposed.

She had no idea how large this thing was that she was standing inside, or how dangerous it would prove to be in its smashed up state.

But looking at the tool laying on the ground by the doorway, she knew she had to go deeper inside.

Because she recognized that tool. It had been one of the ones her father had packed away in his own satchel before he had hiked out of camp days before. He had used it to pry open crates when the lids clung shut a little too stubbornly. It would've worked perfectly to force open that doorway from the outside, where there had been no handle.

As anxious as she was to hunt for signs of which way her father had gone, the habits he had ingrained in her ran too deep for her to be hasty.

No, after sipping as slowly as she could at her portion of water, she sat down, took out her journal, and sketched everything around her.

Sketching helped her see things better. Details she thought she was noticing came into sharper focus when she really looked at them, when she looked at them in the way she needed to when drawing them.

For one, she realized everything wasn't metal, like she had been thinking. Whatever was on the ceiling of the corridor, it wasn't metal. It looked coarser than cloth in texture, but it was definitely made of fibers of some sort. She couldn't tell the color, not in the grayish light that penetrated that far into the interior, but it looked dark. Maybe a red or a purple?

More than that, there was something dead center on each of the doors she could just barely see from where she was sitting. It looked like random dark gray patterns against the lighter gray of the metal doors.

But she was pretty sure it was the opposite of random. She was pretty sure it was writing of some sort.

She would have to get closer to investigate further. But that would mean climbing up that hallway first.

"Kora, are you ready?" she asked as she stowed her journal back in her satchel, made sure the top flap was buckled closed to protect the contents, then set the weight of it against her lower back.

"Lafayette!" Kora said eagerly.

And Lafayette started to climb.

CHAPTER 11

The further Lafayette climbed away from the open doorway, the darker the world around her became. And she realized she had never known what total darkness was, although she thought she had.

Even on the rare occasion when both of the moons were in their dark phases, the stars still lit up the fields around her village well enough to see the outlines of the buildings and, beyond that, the horizon.

Even when the summer storms dominated the skies with massive dark clouds heavy with rain and hail, there had been lightning that lit up the world brighter than the sun, if only for a split second.

And even indoors, when her mother closed all the window shutters and the door in the deep of night so she could bring her journals out to teach Lafayette the more secret knowledge she had gathered, even then there had been light. Even when her mother thought she heard someone approaching the door and quickly extinguished her tiny reading lamp, Lafayette had still been able to see the outline where the door didn't quite meet the doorframe or where the shutters didn't quite cover the windows. It had been a thin, grayish light. But it had always been there.

But inside this metallic structure, the grays were very dark indeed.

And after she had climbed far enough that the slope of the hallway had taken her out of reach of the sunlight streaming through the cracked open door she had come in through, those grays became totally black.

Strain as she might to see, there was nothing there. Nothing but the blackness, and what her hands could feel.

Sounds were strange as well. For the first time, Lafayette realized that Kora's hover disc made a slight humming sound when it was working. Lafayette could only hear it when she had rested in one place long enough for her own breathing to quieten down, but it was there. And she'd never heard it before. But there were no breezes through plants here, no insects droning back and forth to each other, no singing of birds.

But more than that, the feeling like the space around her was swallowing up the sounds she did make persisted. She had to stretch to the very limits of her reach to find her next handhold on more than one occasion, then strain to pull herself up by her fingertips until her feet could catch on something. Every time she made that maneuver, she grunted and groaned with the effort. It was hard work, even for someone like her who had been helping out with farm work her entire life.

Yet all those grunts and groans echoed in a way that diminished all too quickly.

She didn't know what details she was missing seeing as she climbed. She might be missing clues which way her father had gone. She was definitely missing any other places where the strange writing was printed on the walls or doorways.

There was so much to be learned here. But all she could do was climb through the darkness.

Lafayette stopped after several hours to perch in an open doorway and carefully munch at one of the protein bars. It crumbled, just as it always did, and it stuck to her teeth. But she had only a few drops left in her canteen.

She really hoped she found her father soon. And she really, really hoped he had more water with him. He must've found some place he wanted to study more closely, a place where he had set up a camp inside the structure. She didn't know if he would risk a fire in such close quarters, but surely he had spread out a sleeping bag. And found a source of fresh water.

After all those days of camping together as they crossed the grasslands, she knew well what he looked for in a campsite. And a water supply always came first.

Lafayette continued her long climb after lunch, although the climb was getting easier now. At first, she thought she was imagining it. Or perhaps she was just getting used to it?

But that made no sense. Climbing got easier when you got used to it, sure, but that was a process measured in days and weeks. Not the course of a single day. And especially not over the course of a single waterless day with nothing but crummy protein bars for fuel.

No, the slope simply wasn't as steep as it had been before. And once she'd come to that conclusion, the rate at which the slope changed increased. It never got quite flat, but once it went from ninety degrees to forty-five, she was happy enough. No more pulling herself up by her fingertips. She only needed handholds now to be sure of her balance.

Which was important, being sure of her balance. She was so tired, and the muscles in her legs were twitching in random patterns. It would be all too easy to make a misstep now. Even if she didn't tumble all the way back, inadvertently stepping into one of the open doorways would be painful enough.

And if she got hurt and trapped in one of the rooms, she had no idea what she would do next.

Best not to test it.

Lafayette was just beginning to wonder where she could safely camp out for the night—probably in one of those rooms with the open doorways, although she'd seen nothing like a spot flat enough for proper sleeping—when she realized she was making out details. She could see rough outlines of light gray against dark gray. She could see into the rooms with the open doorways enough to know they weren't suitable for camping.

And the corridor itself was filled with gray light. She knew this wasn't just her eyes adjusting. If that had been possible, it would've happened hours before.

No, something was trickling just a hint of light into the corridor.

Something up ahead.

Lafayette had to resist the temptation to hurry, to climb faster, to reach that light as quickly as she could. The only bigger injury risk she knew than being super tired was being in a hurry. So she forced herself to be sure of her foot placement before taking each step, to grasp things with her hands whenever she could to keep herself steady.

But in the gray light of the corridor, she saw that the slope was even less than it had been before. It was about thirty degrees now.

Which didn't make sense. She had been climbing all day, since shortly after dawn until what had to be sunset. And as much as the slope was less now, it was still sloping *up*. She had been climbing up all day, like an ant making its way around the outside of an enormous wheel.

But she had started that morning so close to the treetops she had been able to see through them to the sky beyond. She had been able to make out every branch and every leaf. She had been so close to the top.

So where was she now? And how was it even possible, this journey she'd been making?

She couldn't puzzle it out. As tired as her legs were, her brain felt exhausted, too. Maybe after dinner and a night's rest, she would be able to figure something out. But at the moment, it was just confusing.

Then she reached a point where the light was brightest, emanating up from an opening in the floor to illuminate the ceiling overhead. Unlike the doorways, which were all situated so high off the floor that even when open would require anyone to step into the room beyond over a sizable lip, this hole in the floor stretched from wall to wall entirely.

Lafayette took this in, and then the image just flipped around in her tired brain, and she finally realized what she was looking at.

The hole in the floor was another corridor crossing her own. It was smaller than her corridor, and peering down into it, it had no doorways that she could see.

But the light below was so bright, she couldn't see far into it. Just enough to make out the rungs of a ladder built into each of the four sides of the corridor.

Then she saw that the walls where the two corridors met were covered in writing. Writing and arrows pointing towards any of the three directions that were possible from where she was standing.

The writing was very close to the floor of the corridor she was standing in, or so Lafayette thought at first.

Then her brain flipped the image around again. She took a closer look at the doorways she had passed, and the strange covering on what she had thought before was the ceiling, and she realized the writing wasn't close to the *floor*.

It was close to the *ceiling*. Which was what she was standing on.

Which meant this corridor that was like a hole in the ground was really a hole in the ceiling. Which was why the ladder rungs continued on to the floor over Lafayette's head on the two sides that remained walls and not open corridors all the way down.

She was still very confused. Tired and confused. But she took a moment anyway to sit down, pull out her journal, and copy down all the writing she could see. Then she drew a rough sketch of where she was and where each of those arrows was pointing.

It might be useful later, if she ever figured out what all the letters were in this strange alphabet.

"Lafayette?" Kora said softly from where she had settled down by Lafayette's side. She had her snout resting on Lafayette's thigh, watching as she worked, and spoke only when she saw the pencil had stopped moving.

"I'm hungry too," Lafayette told her, although she had no idea what Kora had actually been trying to say. She closed up the journal and put it away in her satchel. "We'll eat once we get to wherever that light is, okay?" she added as she double-checked her buckles. "It looks close. We'll be there soon. Are you ready?"

"Lafayette," Kora said resignedly.

Lafayette had no idea if running the hover disc all day like she had been was actually exhausting for the dog, or if she was just being empathetic with Lafayette, who really was bone tired.

Either way, they'd be somewhere they could rest soon. Because while the light she was about to climb down to was far too silvery-blue to possibly be sunlight, and too bright to be moonlight, it was also so bright it just had to be close.

Lafayette didn't need to climb on the ladder rungs to follow this new corridor, thankfully. Whatever had skewed this entire structure to make floors out of ceilings and made nothing anywhere actually flat and level like it ought to be meant that this space that was clearly meant to be straight up and down was also at an angle.

She was going down now, but down at about the same thirty-degree angle she'd just been climbing at. Totally walkable.

In fact, the ladder rungs were, if anything, a nuisance. It would be all too easy to trip over them if she wasn't careful.

On top of just being exhausted, she was also half-blinded by the ever-intensifying light. This was a brightness that was so intense it almost made her miss the darkness from before.

But at least she had the soft hum of Kora's hover disc to keep her company. In the space of a day, that had become the most comforting sound she'd ever heard. It was steady, and always with her.

As if knowing somehow that Lafayette was thinking of her, Kora looked up at the girl with a big, goofy dog grin. She didn't speak, she just gazed up at her with warm affection clear in her eyes.

Lafayette was indulging in holding that eye contact when she did just what she knew she would do the minute she stopped focusing on her feet.

She tripped over one of those ladder rungs.

It wasn't disastrous. She didn't even fall, just stumbled against one of the walls and caught herself with her hands.

"Lafayette?" Kora asked, worried.

"I'm okay," Lafayette said after sucking in few breaths between her clenched teeth. She was very angry with herself, but she wasn't hurt.

Or at least, not much. She was sure that her left ankle was going to be sporting some nice bruises in the morning to offset the deep scratches on the right one.

But she really was okay.

Or so she thought, for half a second.

Then a deep voice boomed out of the heart of the light ahead of her. "Who's there?"

CHAPTER 12

Lafayette stood frozen in place for what felt like an eternity.

Which wasn't a plan. She couldn't become invisible just by standing still. Whoever had heard her stumble and heard Kora speak her name wouldn't dismiss it just because they were being quiet now. They would come to investigate.

But there had been no doorways in this new corridor. There was nowhere to hide here. She'd have to go all the way back to the main corridor, and even there, she couldn't remember the last time she'd passed an open doorway.

She wasn't sure if she could open a closed door, either. Not without using her father's prying tool. Which she had in her satchel, for all the good it would do her.

It would take strength, which she wasn't sure she had enough left of.

And it would almost certainly make even more noise.

She was still standing still, her heart pounding faster even than her thoughts were racing, when Kora suddenly did something that Lafayette didn't even know was possible.

Kora said a word that wasn't Lafayette's name.

"Pascal!" Kora called out. And then she charged on ahead, into the light. Lafayette lunged to catch at the dog, but Kora was too fast. Lafayette ended up with her hands closing over empty air as the skittering sound of dog nails on metallic wall raced away from her.

"Kora!" Lafayette tried to shout the dog's name in a whisper, but she had to admit that wasn't really something it was possible to do.

Then she realized just what it was that Kora had said.

She had said Pascal. That was Lafayette's father's name. It made sense she could say both, although as far as Lafayette knew, Kora had never spoken it out loud. From the day her father had shown Lafayette what he had done to her mother's ailing dog, that dog had stuck close to Lafayette's side. Like there was no other person in her world.

Which was always how Kora had been before, sure. But the only person in her world had been Lafayette's mother.

She heard Kora bark at first in joy and then in what sounded like alarm. Then she was speaking again, saying Lafayette's name over and over and over.

"I'm coming!" Lafayette said, and continued on down the corridor. Not that she dared to run. One stumble-induced bruised ankle was quite enough, thank you.

But she did hurry.

Right up until she reached the lip of yet another wall to wall hole in the ground. Or rather, another cross-corridor to the one she was standing in. This too had no doors of any kind, only ladder rungs set into each of the four sides.

But this one really did go straight down, or nearly so. There was a slight angle to it, but not much.

Lafayette was going to have to climb. And she was going to have to start climbing down a ladder without knowing just how far it went down, or how long she'd have to hang onto those rungs with no opportunity for a rest.

Except, that voice—which must've been her father's voice, although the tone of command he had used was not when she'd ever heard from him before—hadn't been far. It couldn't be far to the bottom.

Kora was still calling her name, over and over. So Lafayette took a deep breath, then started down what she really hoped was the last stretch of corridor for the day.

When she reached the bottom, she realized with some relief that finally, *finally*, she was standing on what was meant to be the floor. The fibrous covering was a deep navy blue interwoven with what looked like gold thread.

And she could see all that because this corridor was bathing in bright light. She blinked, but she couldn't wait for her eyes to properly adjust. She just put a hand over her eyes like she had done on many an other day to shade them from the sun. And she headed in the direction of Kora's excited voice.

But carefully. She might be standing on the floor now, but it was a floor that was still canted at enough of a slope to be a trip hazard. At least the walls here were rung-free, their surface smooth and cold under her fingertips.

Luckily, Kora's voice was coming from the first open doorway. Lafayette stepped inside to find the light even brighter here than in the corridor. But it still wasn't sunlight. It was some sort of artificial light, but one a thousand times brighter than the lamp in her satchel. Than all the lamps her father had used throughout their campsite all together.

"Lafayette!" she heard her father say. And that really was his voice, his normal deep but soft voice.

"Father!" she said, and followed the sound to the far corner of the room. Kora was there, sitting on the floor with her tail thumping and sweeping, thumping and sweeping, as if she could barely contain herself.

Then Lafayette saw her father. He looked better than she did, she was sure. He was skinny, but that was always true. He was taller than most people she'd ever seen, save only his mentor, Uche Okafo, but even with his broad shoulders, he was still all lean muscle.

Skinny aside, though, his cheeks were as full as ever, not like he'd been without food or even without water. The tight curls of his hair were longer than when she'd seen him last, but not as long as they'd been in times in the past, when he'd been away from home for long journeys into very remote places.

He also looked like he had bathed recently. And had washed his clothes. He was barefoot and wearing only his trousers and white undershirt, but she could see his vest with all its bulging pockets, his hiking boots and socks all neatly arranged against the far wall behind him. Like they were ready and waiting for him the minute he chose to go back out into the jungle.

So why hadn't he so chose?

But Lafayette pushed that thought aside.

He was standing in front of Kora, but while Kora was in the middle of the room, he was in some kind of nook off the main room. Like a bedroom, she guessed, because she could see a bunk built into the wall behind him next to a sink and what looked like an open, doorless cabinet. But there was no wall separating that bedroom from the rest of this open space. There wasn't even a curtain.

But there was a shimmering quality to the air between Kora and her father. Lafayette was just reaching out to see what was causing that shimmer when her father called out her name in alarm at the same instant as Kora lunged up, caught the back of Lafayette's pants, and hauled her back with so much force Lafayette found herself stumbling again.

This time she really did fall down, back onto her butt. And because she had twisted at the last minute to avoid landing on the dog—who frankly, with all of her father's modifications, could probably have taken the blow—Lafayette landed wrong, too hard on one hip. She felt that impact jarring through all of her pelvic bones, up her spine and into her skull to rattle her teeth.

Lafayette sat blinking for several breaths, willing herself not to cry. She wasn't that hurt. But it had been a long, miserable day.

"There's some sort of barrier keeping me in this room, Lafayette," her father explained to her in his most gentle voice. "Kora already got a shock before I could warn her. She was just trying to protect you."

Lafayette didn't trust her voice to stay steady if she tried speaking. But she pulled the dog close into a tight hug.

"You were supposed to go back to the village," he said at last. "If I didn't come back to camp, you were supposed to go home. We agreed."

Lafayette said nothing, just buried her face against Kora's warm and fuzzy neck.

"Not that I'm not grateful," he went on, the paternal sternness of his voice gone as quickly as it had come. "But I just don't think you're going to be able to help me."

"What do you mean?" Lafayette asked. The choking sensation of tears welling up at the back of her throat subsided as she leapt at this new puzzle to solve. She looked at the shimmer in the air between her and her father. It looked less fascinating and pretty now, more a warning of danger.

It was like whatever made the perimeter fence shock intruders.

It was also keeping her father captive.

Lafayette got to her feet and started examining everything around that shimmer. There was something like a drawer built into the only solid wall between the room she was in and the nook that held her father. But when she opened it, another shimmering field of faint light lit up the back of the drawer.

She closed it again, then peeked around the wall, putting her face as close to the field as she dared.

Yep, there it was. The drawer was open on her father's side now.

"I can hand you things through that," she said even as she turned to continue her examination.

"Nothing larger than will fit inside it, alas," her father said.

"I have your tool," Lafayette said, examining what she assumed was a table since it was flat on the top, although it was like no table she had ever seen. It rose up out of the floor like a mushroom, balanced on a thick stem that seemed to be part of the floor.

"That can come in handy, so hold on to it," he said.

Which Lafayette took to mean he didn't think it would be any use getting him out of the trapped nook.

"I only have protein bars left, and not many," Lafayette said. "And no water. Kora and I split the last of it at lunchtime."

"No water?" her father repeated with alarm. Then he stepped closer to the drawer, sliding it back to her side of the wall. "Put your canteen in the drawer."

"It's empty," Lafayette said, but did as he asked.

"I have access to water," he told her as he took her canteen out of the drawer she had slid back to him. He turned to the sink in the back of the room, and just the sound of water pouring apparently out of the wall—with his back in the way, Lafayette couldn't see what was going on—threw her thirst from background annoyance to the loudest sensation she was feeling in that moment. It was all she could do to wait for him to recap her canteen, then slide it back to her through the door.

Lafayette uncapped it again and drank greedily. But she stopped before it was more than two-thirds empty so she could take out Kora's bowl and pour the rest out for her.

"Lafayette," Kora said in thanks, and lapped away at the water.

"I'll refill it for you," her father said, and Lafayette sent him the canteen back.

"Where does the water come from?" Lafayette asked.

"Some mechanism the constructors of this place created," he told her as the music of running water once more filled the air. "They are in a lot of the rooms if you can get past the doors."

That was good to know. Lafayette made a mental note.

But now she had even more questions. "Do you still have food left from when you left camp?"

"No, that's all gone," he said, and kicked the satchel that was leaning against his boots with a bare toe. "But that cabinet in the wall makes food for me three times a day without fail."

"It… makes food?" Lafayette repeated. She wasn't even sure how those words fit together.

"I don't know how it works," her father said with a shrug and a smile. "But it's good food. It should do its thing in a little bit here, and we can share it. I promise, it's much better than protein bars."

It would almost have to be, Lafayette thought but didn't say. But she was smiling too.

"How did you get stuck in there?" she asked instead.

"I set something off," he said with another shrug. But this one was less convincing. He wasn't telling her everything. He was holding things back because he still thought she was a kid.

"I'm going to need more than that, Father," she said sharply. "What if I set something off too? Will we both be trapped? No one even knows we're here."

"They wouldn't come help even if they did, Lafayette," he said. Then he rubbed at his jaw as if wondering if he needed a shave.

"What did you set off?" Lafayette asked again. Although she tried to ask nicer this time.

Before he could answer, there was a soft sound that choked off in the end, like a single wind chime had been struck and then touched again to stop its ringing.

"Dinner," her father said, and turned to the cabinet in the wall behind him. "I only have the one plate, but I'll let you have it first since you look pretty hungry."

"I have a bowl with me," Lafayette said, and shoved it through the drawer before her father could hand over all his food to her. She knew once he did that he'd not take any of it back again.

She didn't want to eat all his food, no matter how hungry she was. She wanted to share it, fair and square.

But she really didn't want to argue about it.

Her father raised an eyebrow at her, but when he saw the determined look on her face, he gave in.

What he had in his hands was mostly flat, like a plate, but curved up at the sides like a bowl. Lafayette had never seen anything like it. He used a utensil that looked like a spoon but had tines at the edge of its bowl like a fork to shift half of the contents into the bowl Lafayette had sent through the drawer.

Lafayette saw him inhale deeply of the steam that rose from the food. He looked like he was savoring the aroma. But Lafayette couldn't smell anything at all.

Which was interesting. Did that mean that air didn't pass through that shimmering field? And yet they could hear each other quite plainly.

She made a mental note to ponder that more later.

She had *so* much to journal before she slept that night.

Her father set her bowl in the drawer and sent it over. The minute that drawer slid open on her side, she could smell roasted root vegetables and savory beef. And when she poked her spoon into the liquid contents of her bowl, carrots and actual cubes of beef floated to the surface.

But so did thick, dark mushrooms.

"Beef stew," she said, looking up at her father.

"Better than the dehydrated variety, I promise you," he said before putting a large spoonful of it into his mouth.

Lafayette took one cautious sip of the broth. Then she devoured the entire bowl with so much gusto she almost felt like she should be embarrassed.

Almost. Her father just laughed, but it was a laugh that said he understood.

"I did the same thing the first time I tried it," he said to her. "I don't like being trapped, but being trapped here has its upsides."

"But how does that hole in the wall make food?" Lafayette asked as she doled out Kora's evening portion of nutrient paste.

Poor Kora. She wouldn't know the wonders of beef stew properly prepared.

"The constructors of this ship could do all sorts of things that seem like magic to us now," he told her as he scraped at the last of the broth clinging to the sides of his plate or bowl or whatever it was.

"You've seen this before?" Lafayette asked.

"You know I haven't," he said almost admonishingly. "That's why we're here. Because I've never seen this. I've never seen it, but I always knew it was out here, waiting to be found."

"Then why didn't you come here years ago?" Lafayette asked. She tried not to sound bitter, she really did. But if he'd just shown people what was out here back when she was a baby, he could've stayed with her and Momma all the time.

He could've been there when Momma got sick. Maybe he couldn't have done anything about that, but even so. Lafayette wouldn't have been left all alone.

"I knew this ship existed, this one and others like it. I just didn't know where," he said. His eyes were bright with excitement. "All the artifacts I've been finding over the years, they were like clues. Most of them didn't lead me anywhere, but some of them—enough of them— led me here. Here, to the ultimate proof. Not even the Central Planners can deny the existence of this ship. It is simply too huge. They have to listen to me now."

He didn't have to say the rest. Lafayette already knew it. It was where every conversation with him had ended up ever since she was old enough to talk.

"Our ancestors came here to this planet on this ship. Despite what the Central Planners tell us, we're not meant to be here on this world. And now that we have this ship, we can finally get back to where we belong. We can finally get back home."

Lafayette chewed at her lip nervously. She knew there was no one around to overhear them, no one who would get suspicious and report to the authorities. She wasn't in the village anymore, where such talk had to happen behind closed doors and closed shutters in the darkest hours of the night, and always, always in whispers.

But it still didn't feel safe, talking about her father's stories about their ancestors openly like this. It made her squirm. It made her skin crawl.

In the end, she forced her teeth to let go of her lip, ran a nervous tongue over it, then said, "This ship seems a little broken, father."

Her father's shoulders slumped, and he started to look a bit deflated. But he quickly rallied, hitting her with another wide smile.

"Maybe we can fix it, you and I. But even if we can't, there's so much for us to learn here. So much for us to learn."

Then he started pacing inside his little nook, as if the thoughts were racing through his mind too quickly for his feet to stay still.

Lafayette knew the feeling.

But all she could think in the moment was that anything they learned from this ship was just going to be more forbidden knowledge. Like everything her momma had taught her, and everything Lafayette had ever learned on her own from either of her parents' journals.

She really couldn't ever go back to the village again.

That part of her life was over, and she was surprised that the thought left her with a pang in her heart. She wouldn't have thought she'd ever miss it, but now she knew she would. If only just a little.

On the other hand, her father wasn't wrong.

There was a lot they could learn inside this ship. And now that they had an apparently never-ending supply of water and food right out of the wall, they had all the time in the world to study.

And then Lafayette was grinning just as wide as her father.

As tired as she was, this was getting exciting.

CHAPTER 13

Lafayette had left her sleeping bag behind at the camping site on the northern ridge, so her father took the blanket off his own bunk and sent it to her through the drawer. It was light gray with darker gray threads outlining a repeating geometric pattern throughout the weave. Despite its muted color palette, it was one of the prettiest things that Lafayette had ever seen.

It was also incredibly soft. And once she had it wrapped around her shoulders, she found it was also warm.

"Are you going to be cold?" she asked her father.

"Not at all," he said. But of course that's what he would say.

"I can look around tomorrow. There's got to be more blankets in some of the other rooms," she said, feeling a little guilty that she was simply too tired to offer to go looking right away.

"There probably is," he said. "I didn't get a chance to look around much before I ended up stuck in here."

"How *did* you end up stuck in there?" Lafayette asked as she pulled off her boots. Her socks were a mess, particularly the one that had been clawed to shreds across the ankle. Luckily, she had a spare pair in her satchel. One of her first days crossing a mud pit had taught her the necessity of always having a spare pair with her in the jungle. "I think

Kora and I found the same doorway you came in from. It had been forced open, and we found your tool there."

"It was a bit of a climb up from the jungle floor," her father said, both of his eyebrows arched high in genuine surprise and perhaps a smidge of belated worry for her.

"I can climb vines," Lafayette said almost defensively.

"I was thinking more of Kora here," he said.

"Oh, right," Lafayette said. She could feel her cheeks heating and focused her attention on being overly fussy with arranging her boots with her socks draped over them to best dry out overnight. They were her spare pair now, but she still needed a spare. "Well, a few days ago, I got stuck in the bottom of a sinkhole. It was marked as a crater on the map, but it was a natural formation. No artifacts there."

"Okay," her father said in a tone that said he didn't understand how that statement answered his question, but was willing to keep listening without interrupting her.

"I made a rope from some desiccated vines at the bottom of the hole, but I needed Kora to drop all her weight as she held the other end. To be like an anchor," Lafayette went on.

"Very smart," her father said. "She weighs more now than she did when she was all dog."

"Right, because there's a hover disc under her abdomen," Lafayette said. "I'd noticed that when she didn't sink into the mud like I did."

"You got stuck in the mud?" her father asked, that worried furrow back between his eyebrows.

"Not permanently," Lafayette said. "But I remembered that it kept her up enough for her legs to carry her despite the added weight. So once I got out of that sink hole and got back to camp, I started studying the schematics in the journal with all the diagrams on grids."

"And you understood them?" he asked.

"Not at first," she admitted, and felt another hot rush of blood to her cheeks.

"But you stuck with it," he said, and he sounded even more impressed by her tenacity than he had at the idea that she had just figured it out at one glance.

"She can float at will now," Lafayette said. "Kora, show him."

"Lafayette," Kora said, and got up from where she had curled up to take a nap. She took a step forward, up onto the tiptoes of her paws. Then she was floating entirely, her paws paddling the air as if she could swim through it.

"Oh, very good," her father said, bending his head as if he were hoping he could see what Lafayette had changed about Kora's underbelly. But of course he couldn't. Not with that screen in the way.

"So that's how we got to the doorway, and it was still open, so we slipped inside and then shut it enough to keep those cat things out," Lafayette said.

The furrow in his forehead reappeared. "They chased you?"

"They chased you too," Lafayette guessed.

"They did indeed," her father said. He was rubbing one forearm with his other hand. Lafayette guessed he'd gotten a scratch there too, although it had healed during the time he'd spent trapped in that nook.

"But the only light I'd brought with me was out of charge, so we had to climb to here through the dark. We only did it because I was sure you'd come this way. Because we found that tool," she said.

"Well, you were right about that," he said.

"You had lights with you. Did you explore any of the rooms off that main corridor?" Lafayette asked.

"A few," he said with a nod. "I didn't find much of interest. They looked like living spaces, but empty ones. There was nothing in any of the drawers or storage cabinets at all. But I could only get into the ones where the doors had been left open. The ones that are sealed might still contain artifacts of interest."

"You didn't try to get inside them?" Lafayette asked.

Now it was his turn to blush. "I dropped that tool that you found. I thought I'd lost it, maybe even dropped it where it would fall down to the jungle below. I had intended to hunt for it once I'd finished my initial explorations. Alas, that didn't work out the way I had hoped."

"You got stuck in here so soon?" she asked.

"Not directly," he said. "Lafayette, as much as I've recorded in my journals, there is so much more that I've seen and can remember that I don't dare write down."

"Why not?" Lafayette asked.

"That's a long story," he said with a sigh. "For now, let's just say… well, you remember how the other villagers reacted to Kora when they saw her."

"I was shocked by the change too," Lafayette said. "It was a lot. I can't blame any of them for not believing she was even the same dog."

"That's not what I mean," he said. He paced his nook a few times, scratching at the back of his neck as he thought through what he wanted to say. Then he stopped abruptly and looked at Lafayette again. "Maybe you didn't notice it. The younger people—the people your age, I mean—they were reacting to the strangeness of it like you describe, sure. But the village elders were different. Did you notice them at all?"

Lafayette closed her eyes and cast back in her memories. It had been a bad day, that last day in the village. She had just buried her mother, packed up all of her belongings, and was prepared to walk away from everything she'd ever known with her father, a man she honestly barely knew.

But she *had* noticed what he was talking about. No one had said anything to her, and she had known even at the time that everyone was relieved that she and Kora were leaving, never to return. But she had seen something in the glances the elders had exchanged between themselves.

"They were scared," Lafayette said as she opened her eyes again. "Not of Kora, I don't think. They didn't think she was a monster or anything. It was more like… she was going to bring trouble."

"Very good," her father said, barely more than a whisper. "That's exactly it. And if certain people ever saw my journals, or your mother's, that could bring trouble."

"Which is why we always kept them secret," Lafayette said. She didn't need him to explain that. Her momma had told her just that every time she had shut up the house in the dark of night and dug up the journals that lay buried under the kitchen rug.

"So perhaps you can understand what it means when I tell you there are things I know that I don't dare even put in one of my journals," he said.

"No," Lafayette said. "I mean, I guess it means that if anyone found one of those journals, you'd be in really, really big trouble. But I don't know why. And I certainly don't know what it could be that you can't safely write down."

"Ship schematics," her father said. "I've found documents that showed ship schematics. Those documents were, in fact, the reason I knew that ships existed in the first place."

"You know how ships work?" Lafayette asked.

"No, not really," he admitted. "If I did, I suppose I wouldn't have ended up in here. But I knew where the different parts of a ship were. That door we came in through, that was in the outer ring of the ship. That was all living quarters. It was the only way I ever found to get in. Most of the ship that remains is underground. Worse, it's under a ground that is under a jungle. If there were other ways inside, they are inaccessible now. But the living quarters was the part of the ship I was the least interested in. That's why I didn't spend much time exploring there."

"So you came here instead?" Lafayette asked, looking around the room they were in. There were three other nooks like the one he was trapped in, each with its own shimmering field keeping Lafayette from going inside and taking the blankets, for instance. Or getting at the sinks for water, or trying to make the open cabinet space produce more food.

"No, this is where the robots took me," he said.

"The robots?" she repeated.

"Like Kora's central core, only an entire thing made up of those parts," he said. "Imagine I replaced her legs and her tail and her head. Then she'd be a robot. A dog robot."

"And there are robots here?" Lafayette asked.

"Not at the moment, but you should keep an eye out for them when you leave this space," he said. "I was in the room that on the schematics was the heart of the ship. It was the central command structure, where the engines were. I could see the power core, still glowing after I can only guess how many thousands of years. It was completely awe-inspiring."

But then he sighed. "The problem was I couldn't read the writing in the panels. I still can't. I was trying to find a way to turn on all the lights when I think I turned on more than I had bargained for. The lights came on, and I could hear voices speaking all over the ship, although I know for a fact there is no one else in here. Then the entire structure started to shake with a low rumbling sound that just kept building and building."

"I never heard a thing," Lafayette said with a frown. She wondered which day this had been. One of the first days, surely, when she'd still been exploring the sites marked on the map that were closer to the camp.

"It seemed incredibly loud from inside that room," he said. "But it only lasted for a moment. Then the robots came. They are like metallic structures, heavier than their size would suggest, like Kora here. But they weren't dog-shaped or even human-shaped. They were like floating boxes, maybe the size of one of the wheelbarrows back in the village, but with two articulated appendages sort of like arms without hands. They shocked me with those appendages, and then gripped me with vises I couldn't break free from. They were talking the entire time, but it was like no language I've ever heard. They brought me here, put me inside the field, then disappeared again."

"And you haven't seen them since?" Lafayette asked, suddenly nervous at the idea of sleeping in this place.

"No, but shortly after they pulled me out of the central command room, the rumbling stopped. And then the lights started to go out one by one. I could see it as they dragged me here. The lights kept shutting off behind us. Only this light remains on."

"The corridor outside is lit up too," Lafayette told him with a yawn. "But the rest of the ship I've been through is completely dark."

"I turned some power source on that was completely off when I arrived, but it hasn't completely shut off again, then. At least, not yet," he said. Then he sat down on the edge of his bunk, pulling his own journal out of his satchel and turning to a blank page to start writing down his thoughts.

"I should look around that room you described in the morning," Lafayette said as she curled up on the floor. Kora immediately moved to tuck her body up against Lafayette's tummy. "Maybe I can turn all the lights on again, but without making the ship rumble."

"No, I don't want you touching anything until we understand things better," her father said without quite looking up from what he was writing.

"I won't," she said. "I have copied down every example of the writing I could find. I can keep doing that until we understand it. Then I'll know what will happen when I touch the buttons."

"We must proceed slowly and cautiously," her father said, still scribbling away in his journal. "Not just for our sakes, but for everyone on this world. It's up to us to solve this mystery and share the answer with everyone. They deserve to know. We all deserve to know."

Lafayette yawned again. This was the father she had known all her life. Totally wrapped up in solving the big mystery and saving the world.

She had always thought that she'd believed him as a kid. It had felt like she had.

But now that she was drifting off to sleep in an actual ship like the ones he'd always described to her in the dark, when they were reliably alone, in whispers, now that was an entirely different kind of belief.

"What are you writing?" she managed to ask even as her eyelids drifted down, ever heavier as she fought a losing battle to stay awake.

"Ship schematics," he said. "Now go to sleep. Rest up. You're going to have a big day tomorrow. You and Kora."

"Right," Lafayette said.

But she was pretty sure she was asleep before she'd even gotten that whole word out.

CHAPTER 14

Breakfast the next morning was a steaming yellow mound of scrambled eggs, a triangle of buttered toast made from the softest bread Lafayette had ever tasted, and two strips of something she couldn't identify. It was crispy and salty, meaty and greasy, and possibly the best thing she'd ever eaten.

"It's called bacon," her father told her with a grin. "I grew up on it where I was born in the east, but pigs are scarce on this side of the world."

"I wish I'd been born in the east," Lafayette said as she crunched on the last bite of her bacon.

"You have mutton, which I didn't have until the first time I visited your mother in that village," he said.

"Mutton is good, but bacon is better," Lafayette said with such an air of declaration that her father barked out a laugh.

But they both grew serious again once the food was gone. He refilled her canteen for her and passed it through the drawer along with the journal he had stayed up late into the night writing in.

"I should copy out the pages," Lafayette said. She knew how precious journals were. She didn't want to take away her father's and leave him to pass the day without one.

"You can after dinner tonight. For now, you should get to exploring," he said.

"I'll leave you my journal, then," she decided, digging it out of her satchel. "And I have a spare empty one. Yours is almost full, but I have a lot of space left in mine."

"Good planning," her father said, clearly pleased as she slid both of the books over to his side of the wall. "I'll copy out what I can from your journal while you and Kora are out and return it to you this evening."

"I have notes on all the craters and the artifacts I found," Lafayette said, trying not to sound too proud of her own work. "I also copied down every bit of writing I could that I saw on the ship's walls on my way here. But the actual artifacts from the craters are back at the camp."

"You left the perimeter fence up?" he asked.

"Yes. I also moved the camp, though. It's on the north ridge," she said. "The cat things attacked the fence in the jungle, and I wanted to camp where I could see more outside the fence line."

"Good thinking," her father said. "I'm sure I'll have more questions for you after I've perused your journal. And of course, you'll have to tell me all about your day once you get back."

"Of course," Lafayette said, suddenly nervous about heading out to explore. She felt the weight of the responsibility, even though all she was really taking on was what she owed her father. The rest of the world that he was determined to save was just too vague of a concept for her. She tried picturing her village but way bigger, but it was still too nebulous for her to pin any feelings on.

"Don't touch anything," he said, his tone suddenly deadly serious. "I don't know where those robots came from or where they went back to. I've not seen them or heard them moving about since. But they are out there somewhere. Keep a sharp eye on your surroundings. And, as I said, don't touch anything. Not until we have a better idea what they respond to."

"Yes, father," Lafayette said, tucking his journal into her satchel then adding the full canteen. "Kora will keep an eye out, too. Won't you, Kora?"

"Lafayette," Kora said eagerly.

Her father laughed, although the worried lines around his eyes lingered. "I'm glad to see you and Kora are getting on better than before. You were still wary of her when I left the camp."

"We've been through some things," Lafayette said.

"Oh, one last thing," her father said, and spun around to dig into his satchel. He came up with a lamp just like the one Lafayette had in her own bag. "Why don't we trade? I have a multi-tool in my satchel. I think I can find a way to charge your dead one from the panel in this nook."

"Don't break anything," Lafayette said, suddenly nervous herself. "We need the food and water."

"I'll be careful," he said. "I know a little about these things. Enough to know the importance of being careful. You do the same with those robots."

"I will," Lafayette promised for a second time. Then she looked down at Kora. "Ready?"

"Lafayette," Kora said.

"I'll save half the lunch for you," her father said over his shoulder, even as his attention appeared to be entirely on popping open the panel in the wall at the back of the nook. "If you don't make it back in time to eat it fresh, you can just take it with you for your lunch tomorrow."

"I still have a protein bar or two left," Lafayette said. But wistfully. Whatever her father was having for lunch, she knew it would definitely be more palatable than that protein bar.

On the other hand, if she ate today's lunch tomorrow, she could keep up that day later schedule. That would give her endless days of exploring the ship without taking more than the shortest of breaks.

She had glanced at her father's ship schematics before she had stowed his journal away in her satchel, so she already had a pretty good idea of which way to start walking. She wouldn't need to climb any more ladder rungs, since the only thing on the other side of the ladders was the living quarters he had already dismissed as uninteresting.

But there had been a lot of rooms on his map with intriguing labels, and they were all on the central part of the ship where she was now.

She didn't know what a "brig" was, except for that was where her father was trapped now. If the robots had trapped him there on purpose, she supposed it was like the room at the back of the village hall where people who had committed crimes were kept until the local constabulary came around on their rounds. It had a locking door and a barred window. But Lafayette had only ever seen two people inside of it. One had been a bandit who had been captured by the men he had been attempting to rob, and the other had been one of the local villagers who had badly hurt his wife in a quarrel.

After the constabulary had taken them away, Lafayette had never heard what became of them. She had never really wondered, until now. Was someone going to come and take her father away? More robots?

She pushed the thought away. It was impossible to know, and it wouldn't do any good to worry about it.

Although she didn't think pushing buttons could ever be the same thing as robbing or hurting people.

Of course, neither she nor her father knew what the buttons did, either the ones he pushed or the ones he hadn't. It was possible that it mattered.

The room she really wanted to explore first was the one her father had been in. He had called it a central command room before, but on the schematic he had drawn into his journal, he had labelled it "engineering." Which she guessed meant it was close to the engine. Well, her father had said he had been able to see the power core from there.

She and Kora had just turned a corner when Lafayette found herself stumbling back. It was like she had started fleeing before her brain even processed what her eyes were seeing.

Two squat shapes, about the size of wheelbarrows, with appendages almost like arms.

But Kora didn't react to them at all. She walked on a few more steps before she realized Lafayette wasn't there beside her. She turned to look back. "Lafayette?"

Lafayette didn't answer. She hardly dared breathe. She just clung to the wall and waited to see what the robots were going to do next.

But the robots did nothing. They just stood there, inert.

Lafayette took a few deep breaths until she had her heart rate under control. Then she crept forward to take a closer look. But she remembered her promise not to touch anything, so she stopped just in front of them and leaned her body this way and that to examine the robots more closely.

They had glass bubbles on them, the kind she knew from Kora's mechanisms as well as the individual components of the perimeter fence. A green light meant everything was working normally. A red light meant something was wrong.

But these were not lit up at all.

So… off? Or broken?

Probably off. Although since they had reacted to her father's presence elsewhere in the ship, she had no idea what actually turned them on.

She stopped herself just before her fingertips could brush over the end of the nearest appendage. It looked like a vise grip. That had to be what had held on to her father when they dragged him to the brig. The other appendage had something metallic and spirally protruding from it. What they had shocked him with?

She definitely wasn't touching that.

She looked around for more clues, or maybe even some more writing, but there was nothing. The two robots were just parked in little depressions in the wall, like they always stood here. Like they needed to be close to something important nearby, but no one wanted them blocking the hallway.

"Lafayette?" Kora said, tipping her head to one side as if Lafayette's interest in the robots was completely inexplicable to her.

"Just a minute," Lafayette said, and dug into her satchel for her journal.

Which she'd left with her father. Along with her spare. All she had was his, and his was nearly full.

Well, she was sure he wouldn't mind if she sketched in his last pages, especially since she'd given him her last fresh book. She quickly drew the two robots, noting the parts and their relative size to Kora, who stood waiting, head swiveling this way and that as if on alert for anything.

When she was done, Lafayette tucked the journal away, and the two of them continued on the path she knew would take them to engineering.

Once they were past the robots, they were out of the lighted section of the corridor, so Lafayette took out the lantern her father had given her. It glowed with a steady, bright light, and she guessed its charge was full, or nearly so.

That meant if her father couldn't figure out a way to recharge the two lanterns, Lafayette had a day or two before she'd have to figure out how to turn on the ship lights. Either that, or she'd have to leave the ship to hike back up to the ridge. But she really didn't want to do that. She didn't want to go back out into the jungle.

Not without her father.

She and Kora turned another corner. Now the lantern in her hand wasn't the only source of light. There was another duller light up ahead, an almost pinkish light that barely penetrated the shadows.

When she turned the last corner into the engineering room itself, she saw this pinkish glow was coming from inside an enormous glass cylinder that stood on a large table-like structure that towered high above her.

The engineering room was like no room she'd ever been in before. It was like standing on the inside of a tower, with floor after floor visible in that pink glow above her. She counted the railings on the balconies of open metallic weave overhead. There were six levels she could see. Possibly more in the shadows far above.

And the glass cylinder extended all the way up, protecting what looked like an immense pink crystal. It glowed dully, a dusky rose color, but Lafayette knew in her bones it wasn't meant to look like that. It looked tired. Old. Worn out.

It looked like it wanted to be the bright pink of the coneflowers that grew in the grasslands around her village.

The temptation to just start touching buttons, to find a way to fix that sad color, was strong. But Lafayette resisted it.

The memory of the shocking things on the robot appendages was stronger than the temptation to save the crystal. She really didn't want to know what those shocking implements felt like.

The pink glow wasn't illuminating enough for her to see the labels on any of the many buttons that adorned all sides of the table the cylinder stood on. But she still had her lantern.

And the last pages of her father's journal. She settled in to work, setting the lantern wherever she could find enough open space, then standing with the journal balanced on her forearm as she copied every shape of every letter she saw as neatly as she could.

Aside from that central table, there were also smaller tables against the walls of the room. Those didn't look like they'd grown up out of the floor like mushrooms. They looked more like they'd jutted out of the walls themselves, like fungus on the side of a tree. But they also had buttons, and labels besides the buttons.

It took her the entire morning to copy everything down, but she was diligent. She didn't stop until she was done. Then she sat down on the floor with the journal open on her knees as she shared a little water with Kora and slowly ate what she hoped would be the last protein bar she'd have to have in a great long while.

She studied her father's ship schematics as she chewed. There was another room that looked interesting, positioned more forward along the shaft of the ship. Her father had labeled it "bridge," although it didn't look anything like a bridge to her. It wasn't even obviously between two things, let alone looking like it connected them. Still, he'd labeled it in large letters. It was probably important.

But for whatever reason, what was really calling to her were three rooms towards the back of the shaft of the ship. They were fanned out near one of the ladder corridors that led out to the ring part of the ship, their curved shape matching the exterior of that part of the ship.

So far, nothing she'd seen inside this ship had given any hint that any part of it had any windows. But if there were windows, that would be the best view she could hope for. From there, she could look up and see the ring. And just how tall it really was, compared to the trees.

Her father had labeled each of them with a question mark, but that really only made up Lafayette's mind for her.

That was where she was going next.

She tucked the protein bar wrapper into the side pocket of her satchel, stowed the journal and the canteen, then whistled for Kora, who was sniffing in one of the corners of the room, to join her.

"Come on, Kora," she said as she adjusted the satchel strap across her shoulders. "Let's go find a question mark."

"Lafayette," Kora said with doggish glee.

And they continued on through the ship.

CHAPTER 15

Lafayette had stopped noticing the slope to the floors. Compared to what she had climbed yesterday, the canting upwards as she moved towards the back of the ship was almost nothing.

It was only when she reached the doorway of the first of the three rooms marked on the schematics with a question mark that she finally realized exactly what her father had said about this ship.

It hadn't just come from the sky. It had fallen from the sky.

That was why it was listing towards the front end. It had struck the ground and become partially buried, just like all the artifacts she had found at the bottoms of the craters. It couldn't have been buried much, given how tall it extended up into the sky, but it was enough to hold it at this non-flat angle.

But the reason why this thought finally cemented in her mind as she stood in the doorway was that this was the first place she'd seen anything that looked like damage. The rooms she had explored in other parts of the ship had looked empty, just as her father had described them. Like someone had taken everything and left, although whether that was before or after it fell out of the sky, she had no clue.

But this place? This place looked like a child's dollhouse after it had been knocked over by a toddler sibling. The tables and chairs were still in place, because they had that "growing out of the floor like mushrooms" look to them.

But an array of strange objects were scattered all against the wall around the doorway. Lafayette bent and picked up something flat, about the size of her journal, but made of some strange material she couldn't identify. It was hard and cold like metal, but far too light for its size to be any metal she had ever seen. There were a lot of things that looked like it, or looked like they'd been something similar before impacting the wall and cracking, crumpling, or snapping in half.

The corner to her left was filled with smashed glassware, the floor and the walls of that corner spattered in a colorful, sticky-looking residue. Like something liquid had splashed all over it, but then evaporated, leaving only stains in a kaleidoscope of colors.

The corner to her right was in darkness, but as she picked her way through the debris, she saw a rare oasis of order as well as some objects she actually *did* recognize.

It was a bookshelf. Just one unit, five shelves that were filled with books. Some had cloth covers, and others were leather or merely paper. All had spines that were too tattered and faded for her to read the titles, even if they had been in an alphabet she understood.

But these were clearly well cared for despite their age. There were no gaps between them, no room to squeeze in a single more book. But there was also no overcrowding, no books stacked on top of the shelved books.

They were all behind a closed glass cabinet door, and also held into the shelves by strips of metal like little fences, keeping them securely in place even as the rest of the room had shifted sideways into chaos.

Lafayette turned to look more closely at the tables. They were evenly spaced in neat rows and columns around the room, two chairs to a table, but all the chairs on the side of the table closest to the door. She ran her fingertips over the nearest tabletop, leaving trailing lines of clean in the heavy layer of dust. Like the flat journal-sized objects on the floor, they seemed to be made of some sort of metal and glass, only it didn't feel like any metal or glass she'd ever touched before.

It felt cold and inert. Lafayette wasn't sure why she had such a sense of anticipation, like something should happen when she touched one of these tables. But when nothing did, she couldn't deny she also felt a stab of disappointment.

The tables were arranged in four rows of three columns, with all twenty-four chairs aimed at the far end of the room. The place where she had hoped for a window, but there wasn't any sign of one. Although that end of the room was more than in disarray. It looked like it had been smooshed. The ceiling had closed in closer to the floor, but in strange lumps and folds.

Like some huge hand had grasped it from outside and just crushed it down.

All those chairs were facing that end of the room because there was a larger table there, twice the size of any of the others. But as she ducked under one of the folds of the broken ceiling, she saw there was only a single chair behind it. It was a nicer chair than the others, but it stood alone.

Or had. Only the seat was still intact now. The ceiling had crunched down on the back of it, and that part lay broken behind the seat, still attached to the rest of the chair but only by a narrow strip of whatever material it had been crafted from.

As Lafayette stood stooped under the crushed ceiling, she could just make out patterns on the wall that remained behind that chair. There was a lot more of the writing she couldn't read.

But there were also things she thought she might understand. One looked like a diagram of a plant cell, like one of the ones from her momma's journals.

Another looked like a star chart. Her father had shown her star charts, back when she was little.

The image on the far left was a mystery to her. It looked a little like a diagram of a sun and planets. Her father had shown her lots of those as well, telling her that the universe was filled with more such places than she could ever imagine.

But she didn't think that's what she was looking at. The relative sizes of the central orb and the orbiting ones were just off somehow. And the colors didn't feel right.

Which, she had to admit to herself, was a strange objection. A diagram isn't meant to be a literal representation, especially not with things like size and color.

But still. She didn't think she was looking at any kind of solar system. She really wondered what it could be, though.

"Lafayette?" Kora asked her when she had apparently been standing too long in the same position, lost in her thoughts.

"It's okay, Kora," Lafayette said. "I'm just going to draw this real quick and see if my father knows what it is. It's almost familiar, you know?"

"Lafayette," Kora said. Maybe agreeing that it was strange, or maybe just acknowledging they were going to sit still for a minute. She went to sniff at the colors in the back corner of the room.

"Careful of the glass back there," Lafayette said.

She pulled her journal out of her satchel, but her pencil had disappeared in the nether regions of her bag. She set the journal down on that large table so she could dig deeper in the bag, then nearly jumped out of her skin when a man suddenly appeared out of nowhere, standing behind the table with both of his fisted hands planted on its surface, the better to loom over it and over her.

His eyes looked huge and dark. She really hoped they were being magnified by the glasses that stood perched on the very end of his nose. Perched crookedly, higher on one side than the other, like his ears were uneven. Those ears stood out from his head in fan-like projections. His whitish-gray hair stood on end in a crazy halo all around his head, too sparse to cover his scalp entirely.

But the overwhelming impression she had was that she had never seen anyone so pale in all her life. Sometimes Lafayette's mother had cared for villagers who had been stuck in their sickbeds for months before recovering. They had been quite pale when they first emerged into sunlight again. But nothing like this.

His skin looked almost gray, as if he had never felt the touch of warm sunlight even once.

She was still trying to process this when the man leaned over the table, close enough that his nose was nearly touching hers as she half-crouched, her hand still on the cover of the journal she had set down on the table, her other hand stuck inside her satchel. She felt like she had frozen in place, like she didn't dare move.

But he was staring right at her, those large eyes boring into hers.

Then he started barking at her.

Lafayette snatched up her journal, clutching it tightly to her chest as she stepped back from the crazy man. But he just repeated what he'd said before. She didn't recognize a single word of it the first time around, but she knew he was saying it all over again the second time around.

Lafayette didn't need to be told anything twice.

However, hearing something and understanding it were two different things.

Whatever he said, it ended on an uplifting note. So it was a question. After asking it a third time, he just stared at her expectantly.

"Sorry," Lafayette said, gripping her journal so tightly her knuckles were going white. "I don't understand you."

The man scoffed out a word, then rolled his eyes at her.

Then he turned to walk towards the chart that had been confusing her. He had a hand raised and pointing towards it as he walked, like he fully intended to explain it to her.

Only when he reached a place where the ceiling was too low and he needed to duck, he didn't. He just passed through it.

Like a ghost.

Worst of all, Lafayette could still hear him speaking. She could only see him from his shoulders down, but his voice went on and on in that strange, lilting language.

Kora was suddenly standing close by Lafayette's side, looking up at her with doggy confusion.

"Lafayette?"

"I don't know," Lafayette said.

The man was repeating his last sentence again, this time facing Lafayette. Not that she could see his face, but his toes were aiming her way.

It was all very unsettling.

Lafayette lunged forward and touched a hand to the top of the table, trying to hit the same spot she had brushed before when she'd set her journal down.

To her immense relief, the man and his increasingly irritated voice immediately disappeared. She was once more alone in the room with her dog.

"Lafayette?" Kora asked her.

"I don't know," Lafayette said. "Maybe we can turn it on again later and figure it out. But for now, let's see what the next room looks like, okay?"

"Lafayette," Kora said agreeably.

They could go back out into the corridor again, but there was also a door in the wall between the two rooms. It was far enough back that it wasn't in the ceiling destruction zone. And when Lafayette put her hand on the handle, it slid open with only a little resistance.

Lafayette took a deep breath, then stepped into the darkness on the other side of the door, her father's light held high.

CHAPTER 16

The ceiling in this room was even lower than in the first, and the deformity extended further into the room. Lafayette had to walk in an awkward bent-over position, still trying to hold the light as high as she could.

The back of the room was a similar kind of chaos, with scattered broken bits of the metal things the size of her journal all along the wall. But there was no glassware here. There were a lot of bits of what she took at first to be wood, like blocks carved into a variety of shapes. But when she picked one up, it had the same slick surface she was getting used to in almost everything inside this ship. And it was too light to be any wood she'd ever encountered before.

She looked at the broken bits and tried to imagine what they had been assembled into before they hit the wall, but she couldn't be sure. They had been nearly as delicate as the glassware in the first room, and were in pieces almost as small now.

But she saw something that looked like a wheel and part of an axle. And something else that looked like part of a spine and rib cage. Which only made her more confused what they'd been in their pristine state.

The far back corner contained a bookshelf behind glass with

restraining bars like fences holding the books in place. But the books were different. They looked newer, all with the same covering that looked like slick paper. The spines were showing a little wear, but she could still make out the letters that spelled out the titles.

And she still couldn't read them. That was getting frustrating.

She turned away from the books with a mental promise to copy down everything in her journal later. She wanted to take more of a look around first.

The tables in this room looked like they'd grown up out of the floor, as did the chairs, but the arrangement was different. There were only four tables arranged in a square, with six chairs set two to a side on every side, except the one closest to the front of the room.

They were also lower than they had been in the first room. Like they were designed for smaller people.

Or for kids. But not little kids. More like kids just before their teen growth spurt hit them.

Or kids like Lafayette, whose growth spurt had been particularly underwhelming. She had thinned out a little, but she'd never be as tall as her momma, let alone her father.

On the upside, she could still creep into tight spaces. Like the front of this room. It also featured a single larger table, but here the ceiling had come down right on top of it, so low she couldn't see past it. She didn't want to put her knees down on the floor—she hadn't seen any other broken glass since the first room, but better safe than sorry—so she dropped into a low crouch and leaned in with one hand braced against the edge of the table, holding the light out in front of her.

If there had been charts on that front wall, they were all gone now, destroyed by whatever had crunched down on the ceiling. And even floor. Now that she was looking, Lafayette could see the floor in the back rose up in the same folds and warps as the ceiling reached down.

"Lafayette?" Kora said beside her.

"I wish we could turn all the lights on in this whole ship," Lafayette sighed. "We have to figure that out soonest, don't you think? It will make exploring things so much easier."

"Lafayette," Kora agreed.

But whatever powered the lights, it wasn't the only power source on the ship. The shimmering fields in the brig might be tied into the lights there. That would make sense, since they were both still working when everything else had gone back off after her father had gotten trapped.

But the man that had appeared out of the table in the other room? Lafayette didn't believe in ghosts. Which meant whatever he was, he had to have come out of that table. She had touched it to make him appear, and touched it again to make him disappear. All without having turned the lights back on. So whatever powered the table was probably inside of the table, like Kora had a power cell inside her core that she carried around with her always.

Lafayette held her breath, then reached out to hover her hand over the tabletop for a moment. Then, in a sudden rush of daring, slapped her hand down on the table.

She saw feet and legs on the far side of the table. They looked large enough to belong to a man, but she couldn't be sure since the rest of him was lost in the low-hanging ceiling.

As she watched, the man shifted his weight to the balls of his feet, then looked like he stood up from the chair behind that table. Lafayette scrambled back as the feet came her way. She stopped when her back collided with the nearest of the tables, and Kora barked in excited alarm.

The man kept walking until he was standing over her with a bemused smile on his face.

He wasn't as crazy looking as the first man. He was shorter, rounder, and younger, with thick waves of brown hair that swirled up from the sides to curl over on itself on top of his head. Rather like cake frosting.

The one thing he did share with the first man was the same gray shade of pale, pale skin. That, and their clothing. They were wearing the same dark brown pants and light brown tunics.

The man was looking down at her still sitting on the floor. He crouched down in front of her, an awkward movement, as if his knees pained him. But once he was at her eye level, he spoke something to her.

She didn't understand a word of it, but she was sure it was the same lilting language the first man had been speaking to her. Only this man's tone was kinder, soft and smiling. He asked her questions, but not like he was grilling her, and he didn't seem particularly bothered when she didn't respond. He just smiled and looked up as if taxing his brain to recall some long-lost fact before trying again.

The second time he asked his questions, it wasn't the same as the first. And Lafayette didn't think he was just rephrasing. It was more like he was speaking some other language entirely, some harsher-sounding language, although the friendly smile never left his eyes.

He tried a third time, this time in a language with whistles and pops.

"Sorry," Lafayette said when he had paused for her to respond yet again. "I don't understand you."

He nodded and said a few words in the first language. Then he beckoned for her to get up and move to one of the chairs.

Lafayette did so, sliding into the seat that was only a little too small for her. Kora sat next to her, pressing her whole body against the side of Lafayette's leg. Lafayette put a hand on Kora's head to scratch her between the ears, but Lafayette's eyes never left the man.

He was speaking again, slowly, one word at a time. But even as he spoke, he was touching the surface of the table between them. He tapped it a few different times before finally registering a little frustration at its lack of response.

"Sorry," Lafayette said again. "I haven't worked out how to turn the power on without summoning the robots yet."

The man nodded, although whether he understood her enough to agree with her or was merely agreeing with his own thoughts, she couldn't tell.

Then he went to the back of the room, to the glass cabinet containing the books. He touched a rectangular panel at doorknob height next to the cabinet, but again was frustrated when it didn't respond the way he wanted it to.

"Is that some kind of lock?" Lafayette asked as she rushed over to watch him attempt to do something with that panel again. It had no buttons on it, no writing of any kind. And yet he clearly expected something to happen when he pressed his thumb to it.

Lafayette gestured that she wanted to try, and he stepped back with a smile. She pressed her thumb to the panel, but nothing happened. She tried again, leaving her thumb there, pressing so hard she could feel her pulse in the pad of her thumb.

In the end, she had to give up with a shrug. "I think that needs power. Although I don't know why you and your table don't appear to."

He didn't seem to hear her, like he was lost in his own thoughts. Then he seemed to notice the disarray of the room for the first time. He sucked in a breath at the sight of the smashed not-wood bits in the far corner of the room, but just shook his head sadly.

Then he looked back at her again. He put a hand on his chest and bowed over it slightly. Then he said, slowly and clearly, "Yusuf Khan."

"Yusuf Khan," Lafayette dutifully repeated.

Kora looked from Lafayette to the man, then back again, her head tipped to one side like she was confused.

"Yusuf," the man said, touching his chest again.

Then he gestured towards Lafayette's chest, not quite touching her.

"Oh, got it," Lafayette whispered under her breath. Then she drew herself up as tall as she could, put her hand on her chest just like he had done, and copied his little bow. "Lafayette Eloi," she said.

"Lafayette Eloi," the man repeated. Then he said something else that Lafayette didn't understand, but she gathered this was an aside to himself. Then he said, "Lafayette," again.

"Lafayette," Kora agreed, sitting up tall with her long red tail sweeping the ground behind her.

The man seemed to notice the dog for the first time, clapping his hands together as if absolutely delighted.

"This is Kora," Lafayette told him. Then bent over to put a hand on the dog's head. "Kora."

"Kora," the man repeated.

Then they just smiled at each other for way too long.

It was a start. Names were a solid start in understanding each other.

But building from that to other words, to the sorts of words that would help her figure out how to turn the power on without activating the robots…

That was going to take forever.

"Yusuf," Lafayette said, and he nodded eagerly. "Kora and I have to continue on exploring. But we'll be back for sure. So far, you're the closest thing to useful we've found on this ship. But we've only seen such a small part of it yet. We should look some more before we settle down to 'this is the word for table and this is the word for chair.' Okay?"

He was still smiling, but she could see the lack of understanding clearly in his eyes.

"And I think we should shut off your table again," Lafayette added with a sigh. "I don't know what powers it, or how to charge it if it runs down. So we should conserve it for now."

He just nodded and smiled, still not understanding her, of course.

Lafayette tried to shake his hand, but her hand went through his as easily as his entire upper half had passed through the ceiling. She didn't feel a chill, or any different quality to the air. Not like the shimmering fields that contained her father. It was like Yusuf wasn't even there.

But he didn't seem to find it strange that he had been able to touch the table and the panel on the wall, but not her. So maybe that was normal.

Lafayette's mental folder full of things she was going to ponder later was getting a little on the huge side. But she added this one more thing to it, then went back to the front of the room to the large table.

The minute she touched the surface, Yusuf Khan disappeared without so much as a peep or a flash of light. He was just there until he wasn't, in the blink of an eye.

"One more room to go," Lafayette said to Kora.

Holding the light before her once more, she approached the door that led to the third room and whatever lay beyond.

CHAPTER 17

The third room was less damaged than the first two. The ceiling was pressing down in a few places, but not so low that Lafayette ever had to duck under it. And the floor was even, if at the same slope as the rest of the ship.

The back wall of the room was covered with collected debris, but nothing here was as smashed or broken as in the other two rooms. Lafayette didn't think this was from this room having not withstood the same sort of impact. It was more that the objects that had been left in this room had already been of a more durable variety.

Like the metal things the size of her journal. There were versions of them here, but they were thicker, and had rubber-feeling bits on the corners that must have helped protect them when they impacted with the wall. None of them did anything when she touched them, and she couldn't find anything on their surface that looked like a switch or slider or similar means of turning them on. Still, she got the sense they weren't so much broken or dead as merely inert.

If her father figured out a way to charge up that light, maybe he could figure out how to charge up one of these things as well. Lafayette was desperate to know what they did, and what she could learn from them. She dug through the pile until she found the one that looked to be in the best shape. Although they were all intact, many of them had scratches, particularly on the glassy-feeling surface. But she found one that appeared to be marred only by the ghosts of old, greasy, little kid fingerprints.

She tucked that into her satchel next to her own journal, then crossed the room to the bookshelf. It was in the same location as the ones in the other two rooms, but just like in the last room, nothing she did to the little panel had any effect. She couldn't get inside.

The books inside were thinner than the other books, but also taller and longer and more brightly colored. The spines were too narrow for words to be printed on them, but she could glimpse a few letters on a couple of the books that were taller than their neighbors.

She turned away from the bookshelf with a sigh and scanned the rest of the room. The walls were covered in artwork that appeared to be painted on their actual surfaces, layer upon layer of images clearly done by children. It was chaotic, but a good kind of chaotic. Like it was all going to make sense someday, if the little artists just kept at it.

Of course, they were gone now. And Lafayette guessed their paints were part of what was spattered over the back wall. It was more brightly colored than the stains in the first room, although some of it was starting to flake away with age.

The furniture in this room still came up out of the floor like mush-rooms, but they were the tiniest mushrooms she'd seen yet. Only little kids would be able to sit here, and something about the stool-like qual-ities of their chairs gave Lafayette the impression that none of the kids sat down for long. These were chairs that were made to be slipped in and out of at a whim.

Like the former room, this one contained four tables, although there were eight chairs around each rather than six, so some of the kids would've been sitting with their back to the larger table at the front of the room. But there were no diagrams or charts or anything behind that table. Whatever happened in this room, the kids would've been focused more on the centers of their tables than the front of the room, apparently.

Lafayette touched each of the tables, just to test. But of course nothing happened.

Then she touched the front table, and as before, a person appeared out of nowhere in front of her. Only this time, it was a woman. She was tall and willowy, with long black hair that fell in glistening waves down to the small of her back. She was wearing the same brown pants and tunic as the others, but she also had on a few pieces of jewelry: hoops in her ears and bangles on both of her wrists. Her skin was closer to Lafayette's brown complexion, but there was still a pallor to it. She wasn't gray, exactly, but the brown of her skin lacked a certain sun-kissed glow that it clearly wanted.

Lafayette put a hand on her chest like Yusuf had done and bowed over it, then said, "Lafayette Eloi." Then she swept her hand back to encompass the red dog sitting by her heel, tail wagging like mad. "Kora."

"Lafayette. Kora," the woman said with a nod and a warm smile to each of them. Then she touched her own chest with a bow and said, "Sameera Adel."

"Pleased to meet you," Lafayette said at an impulse.

The smile on Sameera's face never diminished, although confusion passed over her eyes. But then she said something in return.

"Sorry," Lafayette said, shaking her head. "I just don't understand you. It's a problem."

The woman nodded as if she had understood that. But then she just repeated what she had said before.

"That's not going to help—" Lafayette started to say, but the woman held up a single hand to stop her words. The bangles on her wrist chimed against each other at the sudden motion, and Lafayette put a finger over her own lips, silently promising not to interrupt.

Sameera nodded, then said the words again. She spoke clearly, enunciating each syllable.

Then she said the same phrase yet another time, only this time very slowly.

And Lafayette's widened her eyes in surprise. She had understood that.

Sameera had said, "Pleased to meet you."

It had sounded garbled and wrong, but it wasn't exactly an entirely new language. It was just a really thick accent.

"I understood you!" Lafayette marveled.

"Lafayette!" Kora said, thumping her tail on the ground as if she too had heard it that time.

"But wait! That means you understood me first! Doesn't it?" Lafayette said, all in a rush.

Sameera laughed and motioned with her hands for Lafayette to calm down, or maybe just slow down.

But this was all too exciting for her to remain calm.

She remembered when she was younger, when her parents' mentor Uche Okafo had come to visit. His words, too, had sounded strange to her ears. Her momma had explained to her that because he was from the capital, he said things a little differently than the people in the village did. Some of the words sounded different, and some were words that no one in the village ever used. But if Lafayette paid attention, she could learn it.

And pay attention she had. She had listened to every word Uche had said in his deep, sonorous voice. And she had whispered her favorite ones back to herself later. If everyone in the capital spoke in such rich tones, what a magical place it must be.

But when he had spoken alone with her parents late in the dark of night, all three of them had spoken in an accent that was even harder for young Lafayette to understand. And even as a kid, she had known this was deliberate. She hadn't been able to understand much of what they had said, but it always felt like if she could just force her tired brain to work a little harder, she would get it. It had always felt like she was so close to understanding.

The words that Sameera was saying to her now, they sounded like just another step beyond what her parents and Uche had used to speak to each other. If she listened carefully and repeated the sounds to herself until they made sense, she could understand Sameera's language.

And if she could understand the spoken language, she could figure out the written language. She just knew it.

"What's the quickest way to learn?" she asked Sameera. Because the idea of pointing at every object in the room and repeating the names still didn't appeal.

Lafayette was in a hurry. And she was a fast learner. She didn't need to tackle this in a little kid way.

So maybe this was the wrong teacher to start with.

And yet, with the other two, she hadn't even made this breakthrough.

Sameera was tapping her nose with one finger, and there was a sparkle in her eyes. Clearly, she had an idea.

Then she touched the back of the chair in front of her and said a word, then touched the table and said another word, and Lafayette felt her heart sink. This was going to take forever.

But after Sameera had touched eight things and said the words, she went back to the beginning. Only this time, instead of speaking them, she sang them. It didn't sound like a proper song, really, more of a singsong tone. But it matched the intonation of the words for the objects she had chosen. It had a rhythm. It even had a rhyme.

And Lafayette found it ridiculously easy to match Sameera's sounds syllable by syllable. It was like the singing took away her knee-jerk impulse to just say the words she already knew for these things.

And by the third time they both sang it all the way through, she knew she'd remember those intonations perfectly.

Sameera must have guessed her thoughts, because that twinkle was back in her eye as she broke the song apart, calling out the objects in a different order.

But Lafayette could still sing all eight in a row without a single mistake. Sameera laughed in delight, and Kora beat the ground with her long red tail.

Then they went on to another eight objects. By the fourth go around, they were mixing in words for things that Lafayette hadn't known. Like the journal-sized objects all over the floor at the back of the room.

They were tablets.

And Sameera herself. On the first go around she had labeled herself, "Woman." On the third, she was, "Teacher."

But on the fifth, she had become yet another new word to Lafayette. She had called herself, "Construct."

Lafayette could've stayed there forever, drawing pictures in her journal so that Sameera could teach her how to say those words in her strange, thick accent.

But the growling of her stomach reminded her that it was getting late. And her father would worry if she stayed out past dinnertime.

"Miss Sameera, I have to go," she said, speaking just a little slower and clearer than she usually did.

"I see," Sameera said. "Tomorrow?"

She had to say that last word twice before Lafayette caught it. But then she nodded, "Yes, tomorrow. Kora and I will be here tomorrow. But I should turn you off before we go. So you don't run down your power source."

Lafayette watched Sameera's face eagerly for how she would respond to that. Did she know she had a power source? Or did she know that she didn't? Lafayette wasn't entirely sure there was a power source inside that table. It was just a hunch.

But nothing in Sameera's expression gave her any clues. The woman just nodded and said, "Goodbye, Lafayette."

"Lafayette," Kora said.

"And goodbye to you too, Kora," Sameera said.

Then Lafayette touched the table, and Sameera winked out of existence.

"Lafayette?" Kora said, her tail still wagging, but in sporadic bursts now, like she wasn't sure what the mood of the moment was. She looked up at Lafayette like she was trying to figure that out.

"Nouns are one thing," Lafayette said. "And I guess we can pantomime actions to get the verbs. But what about the rest of the words? Or words like 'construct' that I don't even understand, even if I can repeat them correctly? This is going to be hard, Kora."

"Lafayette," Kora said, and turned to head towards the door at the back of the room, the one that opened out into the corridor beyond.

"You're right," Lafayette said as she followed. "If I just listen hard, I'll get it. All the words. And once we can talk easily together, she can just explain to me what things like 'construct' mean."

At least, Lafayette certainly hoped that was true.

CHAPTER 18

Lafayette felt like she was walking on air as she skipped back through the dark ship to the brightly lit brig.

But she deflated the minute she stepped inside and realized that her father had been waiting for her, clearly in a high state of worry. He was still barefoot, pacing his cell at a rapid clip, but he spun to a halt when she and Kora burst into the room. She could tell by the state of his hair that he had been running his hands over it and probably even tugging at it as he paced.

"I'm not late?" she said. She hadn't meant that to come out as a question.

"No, not quite," he said grudgingly.

"You left me alone in the camp for days and days," she pointed out. "And I think it's safer here than it was in the camp, even with the perimeter fence."

"No, you're right," he admitted. "For what it's worth, I was worried while you were in the camp as well. You only weren't here to see that."

Lafayette supposed that was true. But she didn't know what to say about it.

Their awkward moment was interrupted by the arrival of dinner.

He turned to fetch it, and Lafayette dug her bowl out of her satchel to pass it to him through the drawer.

He divided the food with his back to her, so it wasn't until the drawer slid back that Lafayette could both see and smell what they were having.

She knew there was lamb in it. That she could smell well enough. But the presentation was like nothing she'd ever seen. The lamb meat appeared to have been ground up fine, then cooked in a mix of vegetables and brown gravy, thicker than the beef stew had been the day before.

It was also topped with mashed potatoes. Something she'd had before, but only rarely on special occasions. Potatoes grew further north than her village, and the trade routes in that direction were more prone to bandit raids than others.

"What is it?" she asked as she slid her spoon through all the layers, then brought it to her mouth.

"I don't know what they call it, but it's one of my favorites," her father said between bites. "And to think when I was a kid and had potatoes every day for almost every meal, I swore I would never eat potatoes again when I was grown up." He chuckled at the memory, then took another bite of the dinner.

"Did you figure out how to charge the light?" Lafayette asked as she ate.

"Not quite," he said with a frown. "I think I see how it can be done, but I need something different to run between the light and the power supply that runs to this wall unit."

"Like some kind of cord?" Lafayette asked with a frown of her own. She hadn't seen anything like a cord, but she hadn't exactly done a very thorough search. There was probably a supply cabinet of them somewhere handy near the engineering room. Maybe.

"A particular kind of cord," he said. "I actually drew what I think I'm looking for in my journal. We can trade and copy, so you'll have a reference when you go out tomorrow."

"Right," Lafayette said. She scraped the last of the gravy from the sides of her bowl and tried not to sigh out loud. She could've eaten twice as much food if it had been available. But she would never dare say so out loud.

She suspected her father had kept his back to her when he was dividing up the food on purpose, because he was giving her more than he was eating himself.

But it wasn't a pleasant feeling, finishing dinner and still being hungry.

She turned her attention to Kora instead. At her gesture, Kora rolled over to show Lafayette her belly, and she checked the indicator on her belly.

"Do you do that often?" her father asked as he watched her through the shimmering field.

"I try to every night," Lafayette said. She made the sign for the dog to get back to her feet, then fed Kora her evening's portion of nutrient paste. "I know you said it'd never run out, but I feel better having checked it."

"It doesn't hurt to check," her father said.

But Lafayette could sense he was thinking the same thing she had on more than one occasion.

What, exactly, would she do if the light wasn't green? What *could* she do?

Lafayette shoved the thought away. "Kora and I found the engineering room," she said instead, digging her journal out of her satchel. "I copied down every label I could find. Maybe we can start working on figuring out what button does what."

"Send it over to me," her father said as he moved to his side of the drawer. "I can copy out what you've done before morning, so you can take your journal with you again tomorrow."

"Of course," Lafayette said, and put the book in the drawer. She slid it over to her father, who took it out, then put something else inside and pushed it back over to her.

"Tomorrow's lunch," he said, as Lafayette saw half a sandwich waiting for her. The bread was darker than she was used to, and had a couple of kinds of seeds baked into it. But the turkey—roasted by the smell—had been sliced thick and generously topped with a milky white cheese, slices of tomato, and lots of dark green lettuce.

It looked a little wilted, but was still so tempting she could scarcely bring herself to wrap it in a cloth from her satchel and tuck it away for the next day.

She was still so hungry.

"The ship must be filled with units like that, that make food," she said as she closed the flap on her satchel and tried to forget about the sandwich. The one was easier to accomplish than the other.

"The living quarters probably have them," her father said. "But I think you'll have more luck with rooms in this core part of the ship than out in the ring. They at least stand a better chance of being hooked up to the running power that's keeping these lights on."

"I saw a couple of closed doors I didn't try," Lafayette said. "I saw the robots, too. But they didn't do anything."

"There are almost definitely more than two," he said. "You'll have to keep an eye out. Always."

"I will," Lafayette said. Although she carefully avoided making eye contact with him. She hadn't exactly been keeping an eye out so far. Although Kora probably had.

"What else did you see today? Or did you spend the entire time in engineering?" he asked as he paged through her journal.

"No, after copying down everything in engineering, Kora and I went to the back of the ship," Lafayette said.

"Aft," he said, raising a finger in a way that brought back a rush of memories from her childhood. He always did that when he was imparting some bit of wisdom. "In a ship, when you go to the back, it's called going aft."

"Okay," Lafayette said. Like she didn't have enough new words in her brain. She shook her head as if to clear it, then pressed on. "Your schematic showed three rooms that I thought might have windows."

"There are no windows," he told her. "Not even on the bridge. Nothing but screens and a few hatchways. Or, rather, airlocks."

"Okay," she said again. "Well, I thought I might be able to see how high up we were from there. But we couldn't. Cause, yeah, no windows. And the floor and the ceiling were kind of crunched. Like they'd been compressed from the outside."

"At the back of the ship? Interesting," he said, finally looking up from his perusal of her journal. "I was not successful in my attempt to circumnavigate the exterior of the ship when I tried. The vine overgrowth was quite dense, but I fear it might be more than that."

"The artifacts in the bottoms of the craters were buried in the dirt," Lafayette said. "Some of them were so buried I almost missed seeing them at all. Is that what you mean?"

"Partially," he said. "But there are parts of this ship that I should've been able to see, and yet I did not."

"The top of it," Lafayette said, getting excited again. "I looked up from the hatch we came in through, and we were almost as tall as the trees. But then we climbed up the slope of the ring, and climbed and climbed and climbed. We had to be taller than the trees."

"Exactly," her father said, clearly pleased that she had noticed that. "The walls around us were quite solid throughout that part of the ship. And yet, from the vantage point of the ridge or from the jungle floor below, there was no sight of it. Curious."

"Maybe I can figure out a way to ask Sameera," Lafayette said.

"Sameera?" her father said with a little frown. Like he was trying to recall which woman in the village had been named Sameera.

"Oh, I hadn't gotten to that part yet," Lafayette said. Then she told him all about the three classrooms, and the different objects and books inside, and the three teachers she had met one by one.

"What do you think it means? That word 'construct'?" Lafayette asked.

"I'm sure I have no idea," he said, but with a glow of enthusiasm lighting up his face.

"I'm hoping it won't take long to understand each other well enough where I can just ask her," Lafayette said.

Then her father's mood turned somber. "You weren't wrong, you know. About what you heard when you were little. When you absolutely should not have been listening."

"What do you mean?" Lafayette asked, not embarrassed at all for what she'd done years ago.

"What we were speaking with each other in the dark of night was an older version of our language, one only the scholars know, and few enough of those bother to learn it well enough to converse in it," he said. "Perhaps you don't remember, but most of the villagers couldn't understand Uche at all because of his capital accent."

"I remember," Lafayette said, raising her chin. "I remember they understood better than they pretended to."

"Really?" her father said, leaning forward as much as the shimmering field between them would allow.

"They thought he sounded... pretentious. With the accent," Lafayette said. "They ignored him as much as they could, then pretended not to understand him when they couldn't just ignore him. I know he kept trying to speak more clearly, but they were kind of rude about it. You didn't notice?"

"No, and he never mentioned it to me," her father said. "But then again, he wouldn't. That wouldn't be his way."

"I thought his accent was quite lovely," Lafayette said.

Her father laughed. "Yes, I recall how you loved to repeat him every time he spoke. And then you talked like him for days after he'd gone. I even worried briefly that you'd never stop."

"Yeah, the other kids in the village didn't like it, so I had to quit," Lafayette said. "But I still talked like that to myself, when I was alone. For a while, anyway. It was like I could speak some other, more powerful language. Like it was magic or something."

"Hm," her father said, but didn't articulate what that little sound was supposed to mean. He turned another page in her journal then said offhandedly, "If you'd gone with him to the capital, you would've had a similar problem there, you know."

"The other kids wouldn't like me sounding like Uche?" Lafayette asked. Then she realized what he meant and went on before he could explain it to her. "No, I would sound like I was from the village. At least at first."

She was very confident she would've sounded exactly like Uche before they even reached the capital, but she didn't say so out loud.

Her father glanced up at her with an indulgent smile. He clearly didn't think she could've done so. But it was hardly worth arguing about now. She had chosen not to go, after all.

And she was learning as fast as Sameera could teach her. In a few days, he would have to admit she was good with accents. She'd have proven it to him.

"I have something else to show you," Lafayette said, taking the tablet out of her satchel. "It isn't working now, but I think it just needs a little power. Maybe if you can find a way to charge that light, you can find a way to charge this tablet."

"Tablet," her father said, repeating the word, but not like it was one he'd never heard before. More like it was one he hadn't heard spoken in quite some time.

"This," Lafayette said as she set it in the drawer and passed it over to him. "They were all over the classrooms. They're for teaching kids reading and other things. If we can get it working, I can learn so much from it."

"There are others?" her father asked as he turned the object over and over in his hands, examining all the angles.

"Most of them are broken, but there are others like this one that look intact," Lafayette said.

"Bring me more," he said. "I might have to risk breaking a few to figure out how they work."

"Save that one, then," Lafayette said. "It was the best one I found."

"Certainly," he said, setting it aside on a shelf over the pillow on his bunk. "With what I'll be copying over from your journal before tomorrow, I'll have plenty to keep me occupied while you're out."

"I really am trying to figure out how to get you out of there," Lafayette said, suddenly feeling guilty for how full her day had been.

But he shook his head at her as if he knew what she was thinking. "Of course you are. We both are. And we'll figure it out in the end, you'll see. In the meantime, Lafayette, it's good to have you here. It was very lonely in this nook without you."

"Even though I have to keep leaving you alone all day?" Lafayette asked. She glanced at Kora, toying with the thought of offering to leave the dog with him for company.

But she couldn't quite muster up those words.

Not that Kora would stay if she didn't want to, anyway. Like it or not, Lafayette was now the only person in Kora's world, just like her momma had been, before.

"Even though," her father said with a smile. "Now, get some sleep. I have a feeling you're going to have another big day tomorrow."

With one last belated thought that she'd totally meant to find more blankets while exploring the ship and had completely forgotten, Lafayette curled up with Kora pressed close to her belly and immediately drifted off to sleep.

CHAPTER 19

n the days that followed, Lafayette explored other parts of the ship. She found spare blankets in a closet further down the corridor that the brig was on. She found an entire crate of freeze-dried food to supplement what her father shared with her from his wall unit. It was always a mystery what the contents of each envelope would prove to be, but it wasn't any worse than what she'd been eating at campsites with her father since leaving the village.

But she hadn't figured out how to get her father out of that nook. And she hadn't figured out how to turn the rest of the lights on.

Which wasn't to say she wasn't working hard. But after she'd been to every room on her father's map and filled in the details on her own versions of that map—she had to draw it up in sections because there were too many details to all fit even on a spread of two pages—there really wasn't much point in spending more time exploring the ship.

No, once that map was as detailed as she could make it, she had gone from spending a few hours a day in the classroom with Sameera to spending the entire day there.

She picked up on the differences in their two versions of the same language pretty quickly.

But the written language was entirely foreign to her. None of the letters looked anything like what her parents had taught her to read and write in. And the different alphabets didn't exactly correspond one to one. Some sounds that took two letters in the writing system she knew were combined in one symbol in this ship's system. And vice versa.

But hardest of all was the fact that this new system didn't show vowels at all. It was just assumed you'd work it out from the consonants. There were ways to mark when the vowel was long instead of short, but there was no hint as to what vowel you were making long or short.

Plus, it ran backwards from what Lafayette was used to.

Still, she stuck with it. And every evening after she'd shared dinner with her father, she paged back through her journal to every sign she'd copied down.

And was so frustrated at how few of them she could sound out even after days of learning.

She'd now given her father five different tablets, the ones with the least amount of damage that she could see. But without a way to charge them up, there was no way to tell if his attempts at repair were even working.

But Lafayette had pretty early on gotten past the idea that she couldn't learn to read without having one of those tablets to use.

She had already found tools stored in the engineering room. It had just been the matter of finding a suitably large hammer and breaking into the bookcase at the back of the room.

Not that it had been *easy*. Clearly, what kept the books out of her reach only *looked* like glass. But she had stuck with it, hammering blow after blow until her arms were quivering with fatigue.

And she had succeeded. After hundreds of apparently ineffectual blows, the not-glass had abruptly cracked in a pattern like a lightning bolt that ran from the bottom lefthand corner up to the center of the top. And then, before Lafayette could even choke up to swing again, the entire sheet fell away in a cascade of square pellets the size of corn kernels.

It had taken nearly twelve days to get through the first book on that shelf, a book so simple it was mostly pictures of things with a single word per page labelling that thing.

But Lafayette was stubborn and driven, and Sameera was infinitely patient.

And by the time they reached the last book on the bottom-most shelf, Lafayette could sound everything out herself. She didn't need Sameera to do more than listen along with that encouraging smile on her face.

"So what's next?" Lafayette asked as she closed the book with a strange feeling of reluctance. She had been charging through all these books with all the speed she could muster. So why did she feel sad that it had all gone by so quickly?

"What do you mean?" Sameera asked her.

"That's the last of the paper books," Lafayette said. "But I still have trouble with the signs around the ship. They don't have the vowel markers that these books for kids do. I have to guess from the consonants and the context, but honestly, I just know what I'm trying to read is a bunch of words I don't even know in the first place. There's still so much left for me to learn."

"I can see your frustration," Sameera said.

"So what do I do next?" Lafayette asked again. "Do I break into the bookshelf in the next room, or do I try harder to figure out how to turn one of those tablets on?"

"A working tablet would be a great boon to you," Sameera said. "Even though these left in my room were designed for the hands of small children, they still have access to all the information that all the tablets have access to. The programs contained within them can pick up where we've left off and guide you through higher levels of reading. But I'm afraid we've come to the end of what I can help you with."

"What? No!" Lafayette objected.

"I'll always be here," Sameera told her with another smile. "But you're ready to move on to the next level. That's the next room. With Yusuf Khan. You told me he, too, is still functional."

"Yeah, I could probably even talk to him this time, unlike before," Lafayette said.

But the idea of building a new relationship with a different teacher just made her feel really tired. She and Sameera worked so well together. Yusuf Khan had seemed patient and kind too, but it just wouldn't be the same.

"Lafayette," Kora said, from where she always sat pressed up against Lafayette's ankle as she sat awkwardly in one of the little kid chairs.

"I know," Lafayette said, scratching the dog's ears.

"You're ready to move on, Lafayette," Sameera said again.

"I guess so," Lafayette said. But a sudden inspiration struck her. "But first, why don't I show you some of what I've been trying to read? Maybe you can help me read that."

"Certainly, I'd be happy to try," Sameera said. Lafayette pulled out her journal and turned to some of the pages from when she'd been copying down the screens in the engineering room.

"Your penmanship is very clear. I'm pleased to see that, since we didn't work on that at all together," Sameera said as she hovered over the journal pages.

"But you see what I mean," Lafayette said as Sameera studied Lafayette's careful writing and the occasional sketches of non-writing things she had seen on those panels. "The words are long and compli-cated. I've tried sounding them out with every vowel combination I can think of, but I still can't make a word that means anything to me."

"This might be something you'll want to bring to Frank Paine," Sameera said. But she didn't look up from the pages. And the frown on her face, already grave, deepened as Lafayette turned to the next page.

"Who's Frank Paine? The teacher in the first classroom?" Lafayette asked.

"Yes. He teaches the higher level students. The ones who are preparing to start their shipboard internships," Sameera said. "Lafayette, are you very sure you copied this correctly?"

"Yes," Lafayette said. "I mean, I could double-check if you want me to. But I'm always careful when I do archaeological sketches. Even my father says so."

"Archaeological sketches," Sameera repeated with just a hint of a smile. But the grave look quickly returned to her face.

"What is it?" Lafayette asked. The persistent frown on Sameera's usually sunny face was making her so anxious her knee was starting to bounce. Kora made a doggy sound of protest, and Lafayette forced that knee to stillness.

But then the other one just started bouncing. She was going to explode if Sameera didn't explain herself soon.

"You should really show all this to Frank, but even I can see that what you've drawn here is a real problem," Sameera said. "How long has the auxiliary power been running?"

"I don't know what that means," Lafayette said. But she counted back mentally, then double-checked by turning back the carefully dated pages of her journal. "My father accidentally turned something on in the engineering room exactly forty-two days ago. He's been stuck in the brig ever since. The robots woke up long enough to put him there, but after that everything shut down except the light in the brig and the corridor outside, and the field that keeps me from getting to my father, and the food and water in his nook. Is that what you mean?"

"I think more is running than that," Sameera said. "It's dangerous to run systems for so long when the core is cold."

"Dangerous how?" Lafayette asked.

Sameera lifted her hands up in surrender. "That's the limits of my knowledge, I'm afraid. I can see these readouts are giving you warning indicators, but I only know the dictionary definitions of most of these words. For their actual applications in this engineering context... well, you'd need an engineer."

"Where am I going to find an engineer?" Lafayette asked.

But Sameera finally smiled at her again. "Frank Paine is an engineer as well as an educator. His talent with both areas is why he's the one trusted with getting the students ready for their internship postings."

"So I have to talk to him again," Lafayette said. "I think I'd rather talk to Yusuf Khan first."

"That would be the usual order of things," Sameera said. "But this isn't a matter of orderly progression of your education. I fear the ship itself is in danger."

"Imminent danger?" Lafayette asked, half rising out of the chair. "My father is still trapped."

"And has been for forty-two days," Sameera said. "No, I don't think this is something that's going to go wrong in the next few hours or even the next few days. But it is something that has to be dealt with."

"Maybe I should go back to engineering and check what's there with what I've copied down before I wake up Frank Paine," Lafayette said. "I'm not trying to stall or anything. I just think maybe something has changed since I wrote all this down."

"I think that is a perfectly sensible plan," Sameera said with something like pride in her voice.

"I'll still come to see you, you know. Even if you can't teach my anymore. Although I still think you totally can," Lafayette said.

"I can help you, but I wouldn't be as effective as my colleagues for what you need now," Sameera said. "But I will be glad for any visits you'd care to pay me."

"Of course," Lafayette said. She closed her journal and slid it back into her satchel. Kora looked up at her, curious if they were leaving the classroom earlier than normal. Clearly, the dog didn't want to get up from her comfortable position against Lafayette's leg until it was absolutely necessary.

But Sameera held up a hand to belay Lafayette turning her off for the day.

"Please, may I ask you a question?" she asked. Ephemeral as she was, saying those words still brought a touch of color to her cheeks.

"Anything," Lafayette said, settling back into the little chair, but this time with her satchel held close to her stomach.

"I don't suppose you know… but still, I'm curious. What has been happening on this ship?" Sameera asked.

"What do you mean? Because of the readings?" Lafayette asked.

"You are alone here on this ship, with your father trapped, and no one is around to let him out," Sameera said. "You wander everywhere and copy things down, but there is no one around for you to ask any of your many questions save me. That is all highly unusual."

"Oh. I guess I thought you knew what happened," Lafayette said. "I don't, really. I mean, I can tell that all the people left at some point. In the living spaces, it looks like they packed up their personal belongings before they left. But I don't know why they left you behind. Maybe because these rooms are crushed. Maybe they thought you were too damaged to bring. They really should've checked."

"They all left? How?" Sameera asked.

"I guess they probably just walked away from the crash," Lafayette said.

Sameera just blinked at her, as if Lafayette had spoken those words in a language she didn't know. But they were all very basic words.

"They walked away from a crash," Sameera repeated slowly.

"You don't remember things that happen when you're not awake," Lafayette said after a moment's thought. That totally made sense. But was so tragic. "Your last memory before meeting me? What was it?"

"I had just wrapped up a day of teaching," Sameera said. "The kids were excited. We were going to be in planetary orbit within a few hours. Of course, there were still years of work left before the first ground-side colonies would begin. But they'd see their new home soon. It had been a very big day."

"And then… just me," Lafayette said. "What happened?"

"I suppose the ship, as you say, crashed," Sameera said. "That doesn't seem possible. I've never heard of such a thing. But nothing else makes sense. That must have been what happened. Oh my stars, I hope all of my little pupils walked away as you said. Or perhaps they escaped on shuttles. There were four other ships with us in the colonizing fleet."

"Four?" Lafayette repeated. The sinking feeling that had lingered in her stomach throughout this conversation had suddenly become a plunging down a bottomless hole feeling. She gripped the edges of the table in front of her to remind herself she was perfectly still.

"Yes, four," Sameera said. "Why?"

"Maybe it's a coincidence," Lafayette said. "But my father has been hunting for the archaeologic sites that tie us to our extraplanetary ancestors his entire life. This is the first one he's actually found. The others are just rumors. But the rumors he's been chasing are of precisely four other sites."

"Oh my stars," Sameera said softly. She pressed a shaking hand to her forehead for a moment. But then she dropped it away almost aggressively, as if forcing herself to set that sadness aside. "Listen,

Lafayette, this makes what we've been discussing all the more worrisome. If that core, besides being in a cold state for what sounds like millennia, was also damaged in a crash, the danger you and your father and Kora are in by staying her is that much more grave. You should go now. Go to engineering, as you said, and check your sketches. Then wake up Frank Paine and show him everything. Follow his guidance as best you can. I hope he can save our ship. But beyond that, he really must help you save yourselves. Go, Lafayette, at once. We've lost so much time already."

"Do you want me to leave you on this time?" Lafayette asked. Sameera looked like she needed time alone to process all that she had just learned, and the grief it had caused her. And now that Lafayette knew she wasn't aware when she wasn't visible, turning her off was robbing her of that needed time.

But Sameera just shook her head with a sad smile. "No, preserving my power has been the wisest course. I commend you for it. Until you wake me again, Lafayette."

"I swear it will be soon," Lafayette said.

Then she tapped the tabletop, and Sameera winked out of view.

"Come on, Kora," Lafayette said, already half running herself out the door. "We have work to do."

CHAPTER 20

Lafayette had expected she'd need to redo one or two of the sketches, maybe.

But when she and Kora arrived in engineering, she knew at once that things had gone very wrong. Maybe even more wrong than Sameera had feared.

There were a lot of red lights on. And Lafayette had worked with her father's technology enough to know that red lights were bad. Green lights were the good ones.

She didn't see any green lights.

"It's probably been like this for a while, right?" Lafayette said to Kora nervously.

"Lafayette?" Kora responded.

"Right," Lafayette said.

It was hard to work quickly and neatly and accurately all at once. But she did her best. She filled page after page in her journal, pausing only to resharpen her pencil with the knife she kept in her satchel for that purpose.

At least nothing was getting worse while she worked. The red lights had a dull but steady glow. Nothing was flashing. Nothing was making any noise.

She tried to find that heartening. But mostly she just wished she could write the complicated letters faster. They were more familiar now than they had been before, but they were still far more complex than the alphabet she'd been writing in since she had been a small child. There were so many more ways to miss a single stroke that would change the symbol from representing the correct sound to representing an erroneous one.

Her growling stomach warned her she was getting close to dinnertime when she finally finished copying everything on the last panel. But she didn't dare to go back to the brig, not even just to tell her father she'd be eating late.

She just ran straight back to the first classroom she had entered so many days before.

She touched the desk and the man with the crazy hair was back, just exactly as he had looked when she'd shut him off before.

"Well?" he asked her testily, folding his arms as he glowered at her. "Can you explain yourself this time?"

"Yes, sorry," Lafayette said. His accent was a little different from Sameera's, but not so much that she had any trouble understanding him. Still, she spoke as clearly as she could. She didn't know if she had any kind of accent herself, but she felt it was safe to assume she did. She couldn't hear it, but she was sure it was there. "Frank Paine?"

"Indeed," he said, still glowering.

"My name is Lafayette Eloi, and Sameera Adel sent me to speak with you," she said.

"You're a tad old for Sameera's class," he said, raising a single eyebrow. But at least he wasn't bellowing at her.

"Yes, well," Lafayette said, shifting her weight from foot to foot nervously. She pulled her journal out of her bag and set it down on the nearest table, quickly turning to the first of the pages she had just recorded. "The thing is, this ship crashed on this planet a long time ago. You've been sleeping for years, I don't know how many. All the people who were on this ship left… well, again, I don't know how long ago. But it's been empty for thousands of my years."

"That explains the gap in my chronometer," he said with a frown.

But then he didn't so much nod at her as direct a sharp upthrust of his chin at her. "Go on."

"Well, I've been learning how to read with Sameera's help, but I still don't understand everything. Our languages are closely related, but there are some words you have that I simply have no corollary for," Lafayette said. "Like these I've written here, for instance."

"You've been to engineering," he said as he studied her writing and sketches. Then his frown deepened. As much as Sameera's frown had been startling, it had been momentary. Like a dark eclipse of her otherwise sunny face, there but then quickly gone again.

This darkening of this teacher's already gloomy facial expressions was somehow worse.

"It's serious, isn't it?" Lafayette asked.

"Obviously," he said with heavy disdain.

"Can you help me fix it?" Lafayette asked.

"Do you have any engineering training? Any basic knowledge of ship systems at all?" he asked. Not remotely as if he didn't already know the answer.

But Lafayette answered him anyway, with a small, "No."

"So how do you propose to reverse the catastrophic buildup of materials from a leaking core? And a cold core at that?" he asked her, arms folded as he stared down at her sternly.

"I don't even know what that means," Lafayette said. Her voice sounded if anything even smaller than before.

"No, of course you don't," he said. "Not that I don't think you can be taught. You were completely nonverbal when I encountered you before, but you speak now perfectly clearly, if with an unfortunate tinge of Sameera's fourth moon dialect. More's the pity. Well, some people find that accent fetching."

It was pretty clear that Frank Paine did not count himself among that number.

But Lafayette forced her mind back to the task at hand. "If I can't fix it, what can I do?"

"Run?" he said.

"I can't do that," Lafayette said. "You have to help me figure out how to stop this."

"First of all, I can't leave this room. I'm tethered to the power source inside my desk. But even if I were free to move throughout the ship, I'm not sure I'd be able to fix this. It never should've been left to degenerate to this condition in the first place," he said, sounding annoyed.

"No one is here," Lafayette reminded him. "But you didn't say you couldn't fix it. You said you weren't sure you could. So does that mean there's something you could try?"

"There's always something I can *try*," he said, that disdain back in his tone. "There are at least five things I could try, and a dozen more, depending on how those five things turned out."

"Then—" Lafayette started to say, but he carried on talking right over her.

"But I can't just give you instructions for you to run off to engineering to try," he said. So apparently he could read her mind. "Even if I knew exactly how to talk you through every possible scenario, I couldn't possibly prepare you for all possible outcomes of what I'd want to try. It would involve split-second decisions. And they'd have to be the correct split-second decisions. Do you think you can make those?"

"Not the way you mean," Lafayette said, starting to feel a little annoyed herself. The man's condescension was really a lot.

And yet, there was no way to get out of this situation without him. Or, at least, none that she could see.

She wished she had a few more weeks to learn everything she could bust out of that bookshelf behind him. She would bet she'd learn at least enough engineering to follow his directions, if not enough to not need him at all.

She was a fast learner. And she had never had to be told anything twice.

But she didn't have weeks. She was starting to doubt she even had days.

"I have to do something," she said helplessly.

"Again, run," he said. "You don't really have any other options."

"But I can't," she said.

"Are you trapped here?" he asked, that eyebrow arched high again, like he was mocking her.

Which made her angry. She balled her hands into ineffectual fists. She couldn't fight the man in front of her. Her hands would just pass through him the same as he'd passed through the low-hanging ceiling. But that didn't stop her from wanting to at least take a swing at him, pointless as that would be.

Then she realized that Kora behind her was growling. The dog had her head dipped low, glaring up at the man from beneath her bristled eyebrows. Since the entire middle of her body was robotic now, she had no hair along her spine to rise up into a thick ridge that had always made her look so intimidating before. But the vibe was still there.

"It's okay, Kora," Lafayette said, releasing her fists and gesturing for Kora to calm down.

Kora stopped growling. But her aggressive posture remained.

Lafayette decided that was good enough. She turned back to Frank Paine.

"My father is trapped in the brig," Lafayette said. "He turned some things on forty-two days ago, and some robots came and carried him away to the brig. He's been locked in there ever since. I can't leave until I get him out."

"That is a problem," he said. But with a weird tone that Lafayette couldn't exactly parse.

It was almost like being presented with a big, possibly unsolvable problem, made him… happy?

"I copied the panels in the brig as well," Lafayette said, turning back the pages of her journal. "Maybe you can tell me how to get him out."

"You'd need a clearance code for that," he said.

"Where would I get that?" Lafayette asked.

"The officer in charge of the detention area would have it," he said. "He reports to the head of security, who reports directly to the captain. Any of those three should have it."

"But they're all gone. They've been gone for years," Lafayette said tiredly. She tried to remember the word that Sameera had used. What was it? Oh, right. "Millennia."

"I'm aware," he said. "It's possible there is a record of it in their quarters. But that is a slim possibility."

"Where in their quarters?" Lafayette asked, frantically turning pages to her detailed maps of the ship. "I know this is the captain's quarters, and this one is head of security. I don't know where the officer in charge of the detention area would've had his room—"

"There," Frank Paine said, stabbing a blunt fingertip at a point on her map near the closet where she had found the blankets. "They would've had dongles attached to their uniforms. If the evacuation of the ship had been anything less than a total fleeing rout, they would've brought those dongles with them."

Lafayette sighed. She didn't know what a dongle was. But she knew she hadn't found any uniforms. All the clothing had left the ship when the people had left.

She supposed she was lucky she'd even found blankets and barely palatable food.

"I have to get him out," Lafayette said. "And I can't use an access code. Is there some way to break it open?"

"That's always a possibility," he conceded with a nod.

"Okay, so?" Lafayette asked eagerly.

But he was already shaking his head. "As little as was done to my personality when it was locked into this timeless form, preventing me from breaking rules and regulations even obliquely was at the top of that very short list of parameters."

"So you can't help me?" she asked.

"I'm sorry. Truly. But I do not think I can," he said.

Lafayette almost thought he meant it.

Almost.

She sighed, then slapped her hand on his tabletop to wink him out of existence.

That didn't really make her feel better. Mostly because she was pretty sure she'd have to wake him up again.

But first she had to talk to her father.

She could only hope after she'd caught him up on her very eventful day, he'd have some idea of what they could do next.

Because running away and leaving him behind was simply not an option.

CHAPTER 21

n all the days and weeks that Lafayette had been living inside the ship, she'd never once gone back to the brig before dinnertime. Quite often, she didn't arrive until after the food had appeared in the nook. She felt bad about that—she knew her father worried about her—but she would get too caught up in whatever she was learning to read with Sameera and would lose track of time.

If not for Kora, Lafayette doubted she would've been as close to on time as she ever was.

So to come back at a run at barely lunchtime, and at a dead run at that, was highly unusual.

She had talked with her father enough about his day over many dinners to assume she knew what it was he did all those hours while she was gone. He studied her journal, having copied down whatever was new from the day after Lafayette had gone to bed so he could give it back to her in the morning, then study what he had copied more carefully throughout the day.

He attempted to get the old lantern from the campsite to charge, or to charge the tablets Lafayette had brought for him.

He dissected the more broken of the tablets, drawing page after page of diagrams of their inner structures, struggling in vain to understand what he was looking at.

And, Lafayette assumed, he probably took a nap or two. Because he always stayed up far later than her, and also was awake long before she was in the morning.

So when she came charging into the brig to find him sitting quietly inside his nook behind the shimmering field, at first she thought he was napping.

But she didn't think anyone could nap while sitting cross-legged with their back so straight, their posture so perfect.

And yet, his eyes were closed.

"Father?" she called softly. Which was ironic. She knew she and Kora had made quite a bit of noise with their feet and paws pounding up the sloped corridor to reach the brig.

"I'm awake," he said as he opened his eyes, then took a deep breath. "Just meditating."

"You're what?" Lafayette asked. This was a new word for her. Which was a bit of a switch. Most of her new words came from Sameera or from parts of the ship. But this word felt different from those.

"It's a technique my mentor taught me," he said. "All the information in my head that I had to commit to memory because committing it to paper was too dangerous? It can be a lot to sort through. Meditating helps me recall things I've forgotten, or more often it helps me remember the context for things I only half remember."

"Huh," Lafayette said. Because she was suddenly remembering things from her own far distant childhood. Times when she had tried to crawl into her father's lap while he had been sitting with his eyes closed just like that. And her mother had always gently guided her away, to leave her father alone.

"But you're quite early," her father said as he got to his feet. "Is something amiss?"

"A lot is amiss," Lafayette said.

She tried to be as concise as she could in relaying the events of that morning, and she passed her journal through the drawer so he could see everything she'd copied that morning from the panels in engineering.

"Do you understand any of this?" Lafayette asked desperately.

"At this point, I fear you know more about the functions of this ship than I do," he admitted. "I can't even get a light to charge."

"But there must be something we can do," Lafayette said. She punched a finger at the panel that controlled the shimmering field. An action she had done more than once before. "Frank Paine said we needed an access code."

"Yes, but I fear he's right that no one would've left one where we could find it when they walked away from the ship," her father said. "I don't know much about how that panel works. Perhaps if I had access to it and could play with it for hours at a time, I might discern something."

"Is that how you figured out how to build Kora's core? By playing?" Lafayette asked. She tried not to sound skeptical. But the idea of her father playing was a bit of a leap.

"Yes, in fact," he said. "I found pieces of what I think was a robotic pet at another archaeological site. The legs were lost entirely, and the head was smashed beyond my ability to repair. But the core was solid. So I had kept it with my other artifacts, on the hover cart with the rest of my equipment. That was years and years ago. You were just a toddler at the time. I originally hoped to make it work for you as a toy or a pet, perhaps. But I could never get it to function. Then, when I saw Kora and heard her labored breathing, I remembered that core. I'm as surprised as you that I managed to get it to work."

"Pascal!" Kora said, as if she had understood every word Lafayette's father had said.

"Where did you find it?" Lafayette asked.

"There are other sites, marked in one of my older journals back at the camp," he said. "The people who walked away from here made many stops. Probably over generations. But I've never been able to trace their entire route, not to either end. Well, now I've found this end. But I don't know where they ended up at the end of their journey. At least, not yet."

"You're not going to find it at all if we don't get you off this ship," Lafayette said.

"I do have a thought," her father said.

"What?" Lafayette asked, her heart beating faster in what she really hoped wasn't about to be a dashed surge of hope.

"Those… what did you call them? Constructs?"

"Constructs," Lafayette said, nodding eagerly.

"Right. Those constructs run on their own power supply inside their table units, correct?"

"That's what I've been assuming," Lafayette said. "But the tables are built into the ground. And they're big and heavy. Even if I found a tool I could use to break them free, like I broke into that bookshelf, I don't think I could do it. Certainly not in time to save you."

"We don't know exactly what the countdown is," he reminded her.

He certainly didn't sound at all frightened by anything Lafayette had told him. Was he right to be so calm? Or had Lafayette just not conveyed the importance of everything she had learned that morning to him correctly?

"At any rate, I don't think you'll need to move an entire table," he went on, and Lafayette forced her attention back to what he was saying and not on her own growing panic.

"What, then?" she asked.

"I'm betting there is something like Kora's central core built into the table itself," he said. "You'll probably have to crawl around all sides of the table to find it, but there must be an access hatch somewhere. You can open that, then take out the unit and the power supply."

"And then what?" Lafayette asked.

"There will be a way to activate the construct outside of the table. Keep pushing and poking things until you find it," he said.

Lafayette could tell how frustrated he was, that he couldn't leave his nook and do this himself. Not that she thought he didn't trust her to handle it herself. It was just figuring this sort of thing out was what he did.

"You want me to bring one here?" she asked.

"At some point," her father said. "But first, see if you can bring Frank Paine to engineering."

"Of course," Lafayette said.

Then she was off at a run again, Kora close at her heels. She sprinted back to the classrooms, then approached Frank Paine's table.

It was only as she crouched to examine it that she remembered that this was the most damaged of the three rooms. The floor was buckled up underneath the desk, and the ceiling was crushed down low over it. There was only a corner of the tabletop still exposed enough for Lafayette to activate the teacher.

But she searched anyway, squeezing herself underneath the table. The central pedestal, like the stalk of a mushroom, seemed the most likely place for the hatch her father had described.

The lighting under the table was dim, and Lafayette used her fingertips as much as her eyes, searching every square centimeter of the bottom of the tabletop, of the pedestal, and of the floor beneath the table.

Even so, it was only on her third pass over everything that she found it. An edge in the material almost as fine as a strand of hair, and currently packed with the dust of centuries. But once she felt a bit of it, she brushed at it with the sides of her hands until she had followed that crack around in almost a complete square.

Almost, but not quite. An entire corner of it, almost an entire quadrant of the panel itself, was jammed behind a buckling of floor material.

And nothing she could do was budging that.

There was no way she was getting Frank Paine to engineering. Not without a lot more time and some sort of heavy equipment, anyway.

Lafayette crawled back out from under the table without waking the construct, then headed into Yusuf Khan's classroom.

This time, she didn't have to spend as much time searching. As she had suspected, the access panel on this table was in the same location at the base of the pedestal as the one in the first classroom had been.

But it was also blocked by a buckling up of the floor. Not as totally as the first, but still. Half a quadrant of the square panel was inaccessible to her. She couldn't get him out either.

"Lafayette?" Kora said, and Lafayette realized she had been sitting too long, lost in her own morose thoughts.

"Right. We can get Sameera out for sure," she said to the dog. Sameera's classroom had been the least damaged. It had to be possible to get her out.

Only, she had said she wasn't qualified to help Lafayette fix things in engineering.

But Lafayette couldn't dwell on that thought now. All she could do was get Sameera out of the table, bring her to engineering, and see if maybe the primary teacher knew more than she was willing to commit herself to.

Sameera's access panel was caked with dust just as the first two had been, and the cover didn't want to pull free even after Lafayette had dug out as much dirt as she could, sacrificing a few nails in the process.

But she still had her father's prying tool with her in her satchel. She took it out, jammed the edge of it into the crack as deeply as she could, and leaned into it with all of her strength.

For the longest time, nothing happened. And it felt like nothing was going to continue to happen, no matter how long Lafayette put all of her strength into it.

Then, with a suddenness that sent Lafayette sprawling onto her face with a shriek of surprise, the panel sprang away from the table's pedestal.

It clattered across the floor, sliding with the slope to pile up with the rest of the garbage at the back of the room.

And Lafayette could see the happy, winking green lights of Sameera's core and power supply.

She had done it. She had freed her teacher from her classroom prison.

Now she could just hope that Sameera and she together could do the same for her father.

CHAPTER 22

Lafayette carefully extracted the core and power supply from the table pedestal. As her father had suspected, they slid right out. Like they were meant to be at least semi portable. They were each about the size of a tablet, if a bit thicker and quite a bit heavier. Still, not so heavy that Lafayette had any trouble carrying them to engineering.

Then she set them stacked together on the floor and examined the exterior casing of the core. It had a few sliders and depressions that were likely buttons, just like Kora's body did. She poked at a few, but it was the largest slider that stood alone on one of the shorter ends of the casing that worked.

There was a beep and a flash of a green light, and then Sameera was there, smiling down at her.

The smile wavered a little as she looked away from Lafayette and Kora to take in the room around her.

"You brought me to engineering?" she asked, her hands twisting together as if she were suddenly nervous.

"You've been here before?" Lafayette asked.

"No, but I can tell that's what this is," she said. "That's the access point to the power core. Oh, dear. Those levels really are bad."

"Can you tell how much time we have?" Lafayette asked as Sameera moved closer to examine the closest equipment panel.

"No, not really," she said. Then she glanced over at Lafayette. "I assume you tried to bring Frank Paine here first, and that didn't work out?"

"I can't remove his core from the table unit," Lafayette said. "I can't get Yusuf Khan out either. But your classroom was the least damaged. It took a little work, but I pulled your core and your power supply out. Can you help me fix this?"

Sameera dutifully turned her attention back to the panel. Then she stepped over to look at another, and then another. But in the end, she only shook her head sadly.

"I'm sorry, Lafayette. I can tell things are in a dangerous condition, but how to reverse the problem is not in my skill set," she said.

"That's okay," Lafayette said. She hoped her voice wasn't trembling too much. But despite knowing it wasn't likely, she had really expected that Sameera could do… something.

"Maybe you can still help," she said instead. "I have to get my father out of the brig."

"I don't know if I can help with that either, but I will certainly try," Sameera said.

"I'm going to leave you on," Lafayette said as she gathered up the core and the power supply once more. It was like carrying a few heavier than they appeared books, a little awkward but manageable. "You can just walk with me, right?"

"Yes," Sameera said with a glint in her eye.

Lafayette wasn't sure what that was about at first. But as they walked along the sloped floors of the corridors from engineering to the brig, she realized that Sameera had seen nothing but the walls of her own classroom for more years than Lafayette could imagine. And all the years that the ship had been stuck here, crashed into the earth, didn't count. Sameera hadn't been aware for any of those.

No, for years and years before that, as the ship traveled from place to place, Sameera had always been inside that classroom. That room and the students within had been Sameera's entire world.

"Where do you come from, originally?" Lafayette asked.

"Oh, I'm not sure how to explain it," Sameera said. "Another world, probably something like this one, where people can live and breathe and eat the living things and drink the water."

"But where is that other world?" Lafayette pressed.

"If I had a tablet, I could show you some star charts. But even then, understanding the scope of just how big this corner of our galaxy is, is a difficult thing to do. Let alone the entire universe," Sameera said.

Lafayette had so many more questions. Like what was a galaxy, and what was a universe, and just how big was the scope of their sizes?

But there simply wasn't time to dig into it now. They were nearly at the brig, and once there, their attention had to be focused on getting her father free.

Free.

"Sameera," Lafayette said, the word bursting out of her before she had even finished forming the thought in her head.

"Yes, Lafayette?"

"Now that I have you out of your room, there's really no reason to put you back, is there?" Lafayette asked.

"What are you suggesting?" Sameera asked.

"I would like… I mean, would you like for me to take you with me? Or, I mean, with us? When we go?" Lafayette asked.

"Oh, Lafayette," Sameera said with a fond glow to her eyes. "I should like that very much."

"Great!" Lafayette said.

Hers had been a lonely childhood. There had been other kids in the village, of course. But none of them had ever been friendly with her.

Her mother had been an outsider, if a useful one.

Lafayette had just been an outsider, full stop.

But these last few days and weeks, spending her days with Sameera doing the one thing Lafayette loved best in the world—figuring out how to do something as difficult but as crucial as read the language of this ship—it had been like she'd finally found a friend.

She had not been looking forward to leaving that behind when the time came to leave.

And she had really dreaded it when she'd started sensing that the time for leaving was going to come so much sooner than she had thought.

But now, now it looked like she wouldn't have to. She could bring her friend with her. Wherever she and her father went next—whether to find the other end of the path he had been following for his entire life, or to some other place entirely—at least she'd always have a friend with her.

Of course, that was assuming she could get her father out.

But with Sameera's help, it just had to be possible. The alternative was unthinkable.

When the three of them walked into the brig, it was to find Lafayette's father not only standing as he waited for them, but with his socks and boots on, his outer shirt with all of its pockets on over the undershirt that he had been wearing on its own since before Lafayette had arrived, and with his satchel packed and waiting at the foot of his bunk.

"Father, this is Sameera Adel," Lafayette said as she set the core and power supply down in the middle of the room. "I couldn't free the other two from their tables."

"Pleased to meet you, Pascal Eloi," Sameera said with a formal little bow.

"Likewise, Sameera," Lafayette's father said with a bow of his own. "How did it go in engineering?"

Lafayette was impressed. As much as she had explained to her father the differences between their spoken language and the dialect that Sameera used, she hadn't expected him to adjust to them so smoothly. Practicing the sounds must've been yet another thing he had done during the day while she was out.

"Not well, I'm afraid," Sameera said. "My training is in early childhood development and education, not in ship functions."

"Understandable," Lafayette's father said. "I can tell you are good at what you do by how far Lafayette has come in such a very short period of time. Unlike her mother and me, Lafayette has never had any formal schooling."

"She is a quick learner and very driven," Sameera said.

Then she turned her attention to the panel beside the shimmering field that kept him trapped inside the nook.

"There must be a way to bypass the codes," he said as she hovered a hand hesitantly over the panel. "A way to get someone out in an emergency when the crew is incapacitated or indisposed."

"I agree, there should be such a thing," Sameera said. She pressed her thumb to the panel, but like with the panel for the bookshelf in her classroom, it did not recognize her presence at all.

"Let me try," Lafayette said. Sameera stepped aside, and Lafayette pressed her thumb to the panel, just where Sameera had pressed hers. Of course, this hadn't worked at all on the bookshelf panel. And Lafayette had touched this panel in every manner she could think of since her father had pointed it out to her as possibly a way to bring that shimmering field down.

But this time, Lafayette didn't give up when nothing happened right away. She just kept her thumb pressed to that panel. She even leaned in on it a little, pressing until her whole thumb turned red.

"I don't think—" Sameera started to say.

But the sudden wailing of an alarm cut her off. The panel under Lafayette's thumb jolted her with a shock, not so severe as the shock that ran through the perimeter fence, but enough to throw her back onto the floor.

The wailing droned on, and the brig's lights went a dark, bloody shade of red. Lafayette could hear her father trying to yell something, but he couldn't pitch his voice louder than the continuing alarms.

Then Lafayette saw what he had to be trying to warn her of. There was another shimmering field. This one started at the far end of the room, at the foot of the place where Lafayette had spread her bedroll to sleep every night.

But unlike the field that divided her from her father, this one was moving.

It was moving towards Lafayette.

With a yelp, Lafayette scrambled back out of its way. But it kept coming. She bent to scoop up Sameera's core and power supply, then stumbled in her haste to join the barking Kora in the corridor.

The field kept sweeping up behind her, but it stopped cold in the brig doorway.

She could only just see her father, still standing in his nook.

Now there were two barriers between them.

"I'm sorry! I'm sorry!" Lafayette cried.

"Touch that," Sameera told her over the wail of the alarms. "That panel there, but just once. One quick tap."

Lafayette bit down hard on her lip, but she did as she was told.

The lights went back to normal, and the alarms cut off with a jarring suddenness. Although they left an auditory ghost behind, echoing in Lafayette's ears for minutes after she knew they had stopped.

"I've made things worse," Lafayette said miserably.

"We'll figure this out, Lafayette," her father called to her. "Nothing has changed."

She didn't argue, but she didn't agree. Everything had changed. She'd just doubled their problems with one long press of her thumb.

What were they going to do now?

"Lafayette," Sameera said, and Lafayette got the sense that, even though this was the first time she'd heard it, Sameera had been saying her name over and over again for a while now.

"Yes?" Lafayette said, running her tongue over the spot where she'd bitten down on her lip. She hadn't split it, it wasn't bleeding. But it felt swollen and sore.

"Bring me to Frank Paine's room," Sameera said. "Perhaps the two of us together can figure something out. I noticed some things in the engineering room that I don't understand, but I think they might be important. But he's the one who would know for sure."

"Right," Lafayette said.

But she didn't move. She just looked through the haze of two shimmering fields at her father.

"Go on, Lafayette," he told her. "Do what you can. I'll be here when you've figured it out."

"But what if I don't figure it out?" she asked.

"I'll still be here," he said. "But I believe in you. Go get this done."

Lafayette wanted to tell him that she believed in herself too, but she really didn't. It was a lot, what she was trying to accomplish. And there was so little time to even try.

She just nodded, then motioned for Kora to walk beside her as she and Sameera headed back past engineering to the classrooms.

CHAPTER 23

Lafayette set Sameera's core and power supply on the floor in the first classroom before touching the table and waking Frank Paine.

"You again," he said the moment he winked into view.

"And me," Sameera said, drawing his scowling attention away from Lafayette.

"You," he said. Not quite a question, and not exactly an accusation. But more than a statement.

"You've met?" Lafayette asked. That didn't seem likely, if they'd both been trapped in their respective classrooms. Unless that hadn't always been true?

They both ignored her question.

"I've been to engineering," Sameera said.

"Hardly surprising," Frank Paine said, sounding bored. "If you can pop up here, you can pop up anywhere. And I would scarcely think this would be your first destination." He eyed the core and power supply on the floor, then cast a glance at his own table, trapped in place if not quite crushed by the damage to the floor and ceiling around it.

"I know you surmised from Lafayette's work that the power that is currently running is drawing from a leak in the cold core," Sameera said.

"Oh, you know that, do you?" Frank Paine said. But he stroked at his chin thoughtfully. "That was most consistent with what I saw. Is there more data I wasn't presented with? Something that lends itself to an alternative theory?"

Lafayette rubbed at her head. They were talking faster than she was used to, and using a lot of words she didn't know. But she didn't want to interrupt to ask questions. Not unless she absolutely had to.

"I've seen the core," Sameera said. "It's not entirely cold."

"I understood we've been crashed here for years," he said with some of the disdain he usually threw Lafayette's way. "If the core hadn't been brought to a cold state, it would've blown the entire ship to bits a thousand years ago."

"It *was* cold, I think," Sameera said. "But not anymore. I think whatever Lafayette's father did, it didn't trigger a leak. It just… pushed it to overcharge?"

Sameera had pressed her lips together and shoved the corners of her mouth up into something between a smile and a grimace. Lafayette could guess what she was feeling, like she really didn't want to be saying these things to someone as condescending as Frank Paine. They both knew how he was all too likely to respond to it.

But Sameera had to. She had to make him at least follow what she thought she had seen.

Lafayette flinched as she bit down on her own sore lip before glancing up at Frank Paine.

Who was indeed looking down his nose at both of them.

"Do you even know what you're saying?" he asked Sameera.

"I've read it," she said, lifting her chin a little.

"In an engineering text of some sort?" he pressed. "A procedure manual, perhaps?"

"In a novel," Sameera said, and lifted her chin a little higher.

To Lafayette's surprise, Frank Paine barked out a laugh. Sameera's cheeks reddened, but she kept her chin up.

"Let me guess, it was *Hearts Cross the Galaxy*?" he asked.

"So you've read it?" Sameera shot back with a smile that even Lafayette knew was not as innocent as it looked.

"I'm familiar with it," was all that he would allow.

"It won awards," Sameera said.

"In its day," he said.

"It was praised specifically for the authenticity of its research," she went on.

"By non-engineers, yes," he said with a scornful twist to his mouth.

But Lafayette could see in his eyes that he was thinking seriously about whatever it was that Sameera had just said.

"It's possible for a sudden draw of power to a cold core to create an overcharge situation instead of a growing power leak, if the draw was small enough," he said, scratching at his already crazy hair.

"The power only runs to the brig," Lafayette told them. "And even then, only the wall unit inside the nook where my father is works."

"Nook?" Frank Paine repeated with a questioning glance at Sameera.

"Cell," Sameera said with an apologetic wince at Lafayette.

"Oh. Right," Lafayette muttered. She kept forgetting that her father was basically in prison. She preferred to think of it as a variation of the day she'd spent at the bottom of a sinkhole, working to get back out again.

It wasn't like he'd broken a law. Only a rule that no one had been around to explain to him.

"If it is an overcharge," Sameera said slowly, "is there anything we can do?"

"Actually, yes," he said. "But you won't like it."

"What?" Lafayette asked. Probably too quickly, to judge by the look of annoyance that Frank Paine shot her way, but she didn't care. Time was running out.

"Fire up the engines," Sameera said in a soft whisper. "With all the engines running, the power system will self-correct. The overcharge will fix itself."

"That's a bit simplistic, but basically, yes," Frank Paine said.

"So why don't we do that, then?" Lafayette asked, ready to start sprinting back to engineering again.

She was getting a lot of running in that day. And once she and her father were free, it was days of walking before they got anywhere where they could stop and rest.

But she couldn't worry about that just yet.

"If we fire up the engines, the automated systems will re-engage," Sameera told her.

"Okay," Lafayette said, but she was more confused than ever. "The lights will come on everywhere. The panel in the brig will function, right?"

"With access codes," Frank Paine said.

"Yes, but more than that, Lafayette," Sameera said.

She sounded so sad. But Lafayette still didn't understand why.

"The robots?" Lafayette asked.

"Security robots? Most definitely," Frank Paine said.

But Sameera ignored him, her eyes focused only on Lafayette.

"The ship isn't meant to be down here," Sameera said. "It will attempt to return to space."

"But how can it do that? It's jammed into the ground," Lafayette said.

"It doesn't know that," Sameera said.

"Oh, it knows," Frank Paine said with a roll of his eyes.

"It will attempt to return to the state it's meant to be in," Sameera said, ignoring the other teacher yet again. "If it can pull itself free, it will. If it can't…"

She trailed off helplessly, but Lafayette could tell by the grave expression on Sameera's face where the rest of that sentence had been going.

"It'll explode," Frank Paine finished for her mercilessly.

"With my father in it?" Lafayette asked.

"And you too, if you don't get away in time," Sameera said.

"Or don't get far enough away in the time you do have," Frank Paine said. "Even if it succeeds at launching itself, if you're anywhere near it when the engines really fire, you'll be cooked."

"How far away?" Lafayette asked. But he just shrugged, as if the answer didn't really interest him.

"You said we're in a crater?" Sameera asked her.

"Yeah, a crater filled with a jungle now," Lafayette said.

"You'll want to at least be out of the crater," Sameera said.

Lafayette nodded, but she could feel her chin starting to tremble.

It had taken the better part of a day to get from the edge of the crater to the ship. She really didn't think she could make it back out any faster.

"Once you initiate the engine startup sequence, you'll have a bit of time," Frank Paine told her with something that almost sounded like sympathy.

"How much time?" Lafayette asked.

"Hours," he said with a shrug. "If you instruct it to carry out all safety checks twice—which you ought to anyway when firing up a core that's gone cold for this long—that should buy you about ten hours. Give or take."

"And my father?" Lafayette asked.

Frank Paine just shrugged again.

So Lafayette looked to Sameera.

Sameera chewed at her lip for a moment, then turned to Frank Paine again. "How far into the startup sequence will the brig panels be back online?"

"They aren't online now?" he asked. "You said they had power."

"The emergency overrides aren't functioning," Sameera said.

"I really don't know," he said.

"When the lights come on?" Lafayette asked. "Or later? How much later?"

"I don't know," he said again, stressing each word separately. Then he sighed. "Listen, kid. Your business is going to be starting this sequence running, and then getting the hell out of here. Do you understand me?"

"Yeah," Lafayette said, although in truth, she didn't know what "hell" meant. But she was pretty sure she got his gist.

"I will explain everything to your father," Sameera told her. "We'll go there now and tell him. It's possible that the panel he has access to inside his cell will recognize an emergency override once that system is back online. Then he can simply let himself out and follow you."

"Follow you, kid. Got it?" Frank Paine said. "Because you'll already be running to get clear of the blast zone. You and your weird dog thing both."

"Lafayette!" Kora said, and thumped her tail hard against the dusty floor.

"There really isn't a way to take care of this overcharge thing slower?" Lafayette asked.

"Sure. You can leave it like it is. It'll sort itself out on its own time, sooner or later," Frank Paine said.

Lafayette's stupid heart started to rise up at his words before she realized from his tone that he was being sarcastic.

"Sort itself out still means it'll blow up, doesn't it?" she guessed.

"Ignore him, Lafayette," Sameera said. "Let's go tell your father what's going to be happening. Then we'll head to engineering and get it all started."

Lafayette didn't trust herself to speak at that moment, so she just nodded.

Then she looked at Frank Paine. "Do you want me to turn you back off?"

"So, what? You can preserve my power supply?" he asked, his customary disdain back in his voice. "Kid, my power supply is going to outlast this ship no matter what happens next."

"On or off, Frank?" Sameera asked. It was hard to tell for sure, but Lafayette thought that Sameera might be starting to sound a little testy herself.

But Frank Paine just barked out another laugh. "On, if you please. However this turns out, I would appreciate being aware as I meet my fate."

"Very well, then," Sameera said, folding her hands together over her stomach but not quite giving him one of her polite little bows.

Then Frank Paine looked at Lafayette. His expression seemed odd at first, but Lafayette realized that was only because he was angling his face to actually look at her, to look at her directly and not down his nose to her.

"Lafayette Eloi, it has been a genuine pleasure making your acquaintance," he said. "I slept too long. Even if the rest of my days are endless in number and I remain trapped here in this room with no working systems to access to amuse my mind, and even if my remaining time can be measured in a few paltry hours, either way, you have my deepest thanks for waking me."

"Oh," Lafayette said, and swallowed down yet another emotion, this one some strange mix of pleased and embarrassed. "You're quite welcome."

"Now get on with it," Frank Paine said, turning his back on the two of them and the still tail-wagging Kora with a dismissive wave of his hand.

"You know how to do what he said?" Lafayette whispered to Sameera as they headed to the door.

"Yes," Sameera said. "I know what to do."

CHAPTER 24

Lafayette remembered only when she reached the doorway that there were now two shimmering fields between her and her father. She had to stand all the way to the right of the corridor doorway, and he stood against his bunk all the way to the left of the opening of his cell, and even then they could only barely see each other.

They certainly couldn't touch each other.

She didn't want to tell him goodbye in the first place. She definitely didn't want to do it this way.

"Lafayette," he said, raising a hand as if to reach out to her, but retracting it at once with a hiss when his palm brushed against the shimmering field.

"Dad," Lafayette said.

That word had just wrenched itself out of her. She hadn't meant to say it. She hadn't actually called him that since she was twelve.

Not that anything major had happened when she was twelve. It was just at about that age she started to get annoyed with him for being away more than he was home.

And that annoyance had grown into anger when she reached her teens.

And the anger had not only lingered, it had been about the only thing she had felt for days after her mother had died.

But then she had just gotten too tired to still be angry with him all the time. By the time he finally came home to fetch her, that anger had quieted back down to her older annoyance.

The annoyance had lingered. He had interfered with Kora's desire to fade away, to die and lie buried beside Lafayette's mother. And he had interfered in a way that had upset the entire village.

Not that Lafayette had ever really wanted to stay there. But what he did had taken away the only choice she had over her own fate. She had gone with him, swearing to herself she'd prove herself helpful to his work and learn all she could.

But she had never stopped calling him the more formal "father." Even when she could see the little flinch he made every time she said it.

Now, when he heard her call him "dad" again, even through the shimmering fields between them she could see the shine of tears in his eyes.

"You have to go," he said.

"That's what I came here to tell you," she said, but he interrupted her.

"No, that's what *I'm* telling *you*. You have to go," he said. "I can feel something different in the air. Something is happening. Unless you have access codes to release me right now, I need you and Kora to get away from this ship as fast as you can. No more trying to fix this. Do you hear?"

"Yeah, Dad," Lafayette said. "But listen. Sameera is going with us to engineering first," she said.

"No—" he tried to put in, but she kept talking right over him.

"We are going to try something that might keep the ship from blowing up. Or it might make it blow up anyway. But it's supposed to make the ship go back up into the sky. Into orbit," she said, looking to Sameera, who nodded. She was using the right words to explain it.

"You need to run," her father said again. He sounded so very tired.

"We will," Lafayette promised. "I just needed to tell you. There's a panel on your side of the wall by the drawer."

"I've seen it. It doesn't do anything," he said.

"It's meant to be used for communications, to summon a guard," Sameera said. "It also has an emergency function, to let you out of your cell in the event of a ship-wide catastrophe."

"Right. But it's not functioning," he said again.

"Not at the moment, but after we reset the systems in engineering, things will start working again," Lafayette said.

"One system at a time, and we don't know the order. But at some point that panel will be responsive. And as the ship is already in a state of emergency, it *will* let you out," Sameera said.

"So Kora and I are going to run as fast as we can back to the campsite on the ridge," Lafayette said. "But you have to promise me that as soon as that field can come down, you take it down and come running after us."

"I will. Of course I will," he said. "I'll be right behind you, just as quick as I can."

Lafayette felt a hard lump rising in her throat. He sounded like he really, truly believed that that was what was going to happen.

But Lafayette couldn't bring herself to believe it, too. She just knew in her heart that after losing one parent a few months before, she was about to lose the other one. There would be nothing left for her. Just Kora.

Kora, and Sameera, and a road to the north.

"Lafayette, listen to me," her father said, once again trying to lean closer to her but remembering the field at the last second. "This ship was one of five. Do you remember that?"

"Sameera said so too," Lafayette said.

"Yes, she knows there were five up in space. But I'm telling you, all five came down out of the sky on the same day. I've read the records. I wrote as much of it as I could remember in my journal, but it's in here with me."

Lafayette tried to speak past that lump, but couldn't do it.

"It doesn't matter," he said firmly, as if he could read her thoughts on her face without her having to speak them. "When I get out, I'll bring them with me. You'll have all the time in the world to pore over them."

Lafayette nodded numbly.

"Even if I don't get it, it still doesn't matter," he said. "You know where you have to go next, even if it's without me, don't you?"

Lafayette swallowed hard, twice. Then she managed to grit out the words, "Uche Okafo."

"That's right," he said, his entire face beaming proudly at her. "Everything I know I learned, and everything I learned was at the knee of Uche Okafo. He will teach you, just as he taught me and your mother."

"I'll find him," Lafayette said, curling her hands into fists.

"Finding him won't be hard. But, Lafayette, you have to be careful. You and I, we aren't the only ones who know about those ships. We're just the only ones who know who aren't *supposed* to know."

"What?" Lafayette asked.

"Your village was as far from the central government as your mother could take you, but Uche Okafo is in the capital. And that is the heart of the government. I know you don't really know what that means. Suffice it to say, they are people who very much don't want anyone to know what you know. They will stop you if you try to tell others. More than that, if they even suspect that you know what you do, they will try to hurt you."

"What villainy is this?" Sameera gasped.

Lafayette's father sent her a mournful glance. "A lot has changed since your day." Then he fixed his eyes back on Lafayette. "Trust no one save Uche with what you've seen here. But find him at once. He can keep you safe."

"I will be with her as well," Sameera said.

"I appreciate that. But you'll have to stay hidden," he told her. "There is nothing like you, even in the capital."

"I see," Sameera said, looking crestfallen.

"What about Kora?" Lafayette asked with more nervousness than she'd ever have expected she'd have about possibly being separated from her mother's dog.

"Kora is unusual, but not impossible to explain," her father said. "You've studied her schematics. You can explain to anyone who asks how she functions. They won't think it's magic. Unless they are truly great fools."

"I tell people she's just a machine," Lafayette said, looking down at Kora. Kora looked up at her, tongue lolling and tail swishing across the floor behind her.

"A machine that you built yourself," he said. "Best not to mention me either."

"But you'll be with me," Lafayette said in a small voice.

"Yes, I'll be with you," he said with as much of a smile as he could muster.

Now neither of them were believing it.

"The panel to control that field is one of the more essential controls," Sameera said. "It should come online before things get too dire."

"I'm sure you are correct," he said. "But we've lingered here long enough."

"We'll wait for you on the ridge," Lafayette said, raising her chin in much the same manner as she had seen Sameera do before, when they'd been talking to Frank Paine. "Then we'll go to the capital together. And we'll find a way to tell everyone what we know. Because it isn't some secret to be hidden away, the existence of these ships. It's part of our shared heritage. Everyone should know."

Her father gave her a sad smile. Sad, and yet proud at the same time. How many times when she was small had he told her some variation on those same words? So many times. He had stopped trying at about the same point she had started calling him "father" all the time.

"I love you, Dad," Lafayette said.

"I love you too, Lafayette," he said.

Then he stepped back from the shimmering field, a deliberately large step back. "Go now. Run."

Lafayette nodded, clutched Sameera's core and power supply tightly to her chest, then ran for engineering.

Behind her, she could hear Kora say one last mournful, "Pascal."

But then the dog's paws were galloping behind her.

In the end, it went almost too smoothly. Sameera only had to have Lafayette touch a few things that she wasn't programmed to interact with herself. Then the various screens started to change, and a different sort of alarm sound started droning.

"What happens now?" Lafayette asked, looking from screen to screen. Some were showing charts she couldn't read, others were filling ever more rapidly with text that scrolled by far too quickly for her to even attempt to read.

"Now you run," Sameera said.

The first part was easy, through the sloped corridors of the central part of the ship.

But then they reached the bottoms of the ladders.

"I'll have to stuff you in my satchel," Lafayette said. It took both arms to carry the core and power supply, and she would need both of those arms to climb those ladders.

"Of course. It will be easier to power me off. I'll be there when you wake me again," Sameera said.

Lafayette thought there was just a hint of nervousness in Sameera's eyes and tone, but she did her best to ignore it. They were all nervous. Of course they were. Even Kora seemed extra jumpy, peering down corridors that had remained empty the entire time they'd been on the ship.

There wasn't much left in her satchel since she'd given her spare journal to her father, and she had eaten all the rations she had brought with her. Even so, the core and the power supply barely fit inside the bag. And once they were in there, their weight pulled the strap down hard against Lafayette's neck.

This wasn't going to be comfortable at all. Especially not since she was in a hurry.

But the tone of the alarm sounds shifted yet again. Lafayette assumed every tone carried a different meaning, but she had no way of knowing if this new one was meant to be more or less alarming than the last.

Not that it mattered. She already knew the clock was ticking.

She grasped the rungs of the ladder and started hustling up as quickly as she could. And tried not to resent Kora's effortless glide too much.

Then they were in the darkness in the wheel of the ship. She could make faster time than before, now that she knew there wasn't going to be anything suddenly in her way until she reached the hatch far below.

But climbing down still felt more dangerous than climbing up had. Perhaps it was only because of that hurry, but every shift of foothold or handhold that Lafayette made felt so much more likely to send her plummeting down than it ever had climbing up.

If only she could stop herself from trying to look down. But she just couldn't. The darkness was so absolute, she longed for any hint of sunlight below.

And yet, every time she saw her own feet below her, and then no real sense of what was below her feet, her stomach did another sickening little flip-flop.

The ship was so much larger than anything she could ever have imagined before she'd come inside of it. How could it ever have gotten lost, even at the bottom of a jungle-filled crater out in the middle of nowhere?

And just how powerful was this government her father spoke of, if they had succeeded for so many lifetimes to keep such an immense thing a secret?

The thought gave Lafayette another shiver of dread, but she never stopped her steady pace down the curve of the ship, towards escape.

She just had to make it in time. She just had to.

CHAPTER 25

Lafayette knew from the tight pain in her belly that it was long past dinnertime. Her arms were shaking so badly it was hard to be sure of her handholds. She was breathing as steadily as she could, forcing her panic to stay at bay.

But she was so very afraid of falling.

Then she really did stumble, but only because she'd reached the end of the corridor. She was at the place where the floor bent at the odd angle, away from the endless wheel of the central corridor and towards the hatch.

She hadn't realized she had reached her destination because it was still pitch dark. She only had a vague sense of where Kora was, still levitating, but clearly having been waiting at the bottom of the slope for Lafayette to catch up.

Lafayette longed to camp here like she'd done before. To sit down with her back against the closed door and rest just a little. She had no food save Kora's nutrient paste—which wouldn't nourish Lafayette at all—and she had no water. But just a moment's rest would be enough.

Just a single moment without the heaviness of her satchel dragging against the side of her neck.

But she didn't have that moment. So she just switched the strap from one shoulder to the other, then grasped the edge of the door to force it to open enough for her and Kora to slip through.

It was dark at the bottom of the slope because it was night outside. She knew she had missed dinner, but she hadn't realized by how much. It must've passed hours ago, to judge by how high the two moons were in the sky.

And she still had to get away from the ship. She couldn't wait for the safety of dawn to start crossing the jungle.

She couldn't even wait in the hopes that her father was already on his way towards her. As much as she wanted to.

"Come on, Kora," Lafayette said grimly, and slid through the opening in the hatch.

The nook beyond smelled of cat urine, but it definitely wasn't the old cat urine from before. It was fresh, and so very much more intense. As if every night since they'd lost track of her here, they'd come back to mark the area anew. To keep the warning clear.

Lafayette didn't need the reminder that the cat things would be out there. She hadn't stopped thinking about them since she'd started climbing down the corridor hours before. The memories of their screams lingered in her mind as vividly as the smell of their pee.

But there was no sign of them now. Perhaps they sensed something going on inside the ship, or perhaps Lafayette had just gotten lucky.

She didn't want to count on either, though. She wanted to get moving, as fast as she could.

The first step was one last climb down the vines to the jungle floor below.

"Lafayette," Kora said softly, as if she were afraid of being overheard.

"Do you sense something out there?" Lafayette whispered back to her. She remembered how she had nearly gotten jumped before. When the cat things had been hiding in the trees.

"Lafayette," Kora said. Which sounded like a no, but not a positive no.

But there was nothing else to be done. She had to get down, and the only way down was climbing the vines. She would be vulnerable, easy to see against the background of the vines and incapable of defending herself while she needed both hands and both feet for the task of climbing.

On top of that, her arms were still shaking from her last climb.

"Let's make this quick," Lafayette said, and sat on the metal edge of the space outside the hatch.

She could feel something she never had before, like a low sort of vibration coming from the metal beneath her. Coming from the entire ship. And now that she was still and paying attention to it, she could swear she also heard a rumbling. Softly, more felt in her chest than properly heard, but there all the same.

She took one last deep breath and focused on her firm hope that her father was even now racing his way to catch up with her.

Then she swung her legs over and began the climb down to the jungle floor.

The vines were a little more difficult to climb than the interior of the ship had been. Nothing inside the ship had ever broken away with a snap when she put her weight on it, for one.

But the vines were also swaying with her movement, the leaves rustling against each other, almost twinkling as their motion changed the way their shiny surfaces reflected the light from the two moons.

She felt so very exposed.

But Kora stayed close beside her, slowly levitating down with her paws making needless swimming motions in the air. She had her back to the wall of vines, her nose constantly sniffing at the air and her ears perked as high up as Lafayette had ever seen them.

Nothing was going to sneak up on them. Not while Kora was on alert.

Lafayette was just starting to think she could see hints of the jungle floor below despite the impenetrable gloom of everything down here under the canopy at night, when she must've let her attention slip from her climbing for a split second too long. The vine she had just put her foot down on had felt solid when she'd probed for it, but now that she lowered herself onto it, it snapped with unexpected ferocity. The end below her slithered away into the darkness, but the end above her foot whipped back up at her, smacking her across the thigh with enough force to make her hiss with pain.

Then the vine under her other foot started to give way. She scrambled to secure her handholds, but before she could move her right hand to a thicker vine, both of her feet were dangling free and she was hanging by her fingertips.

The ground wasn't far below her; she knew that. But a fall from two meters and a fall from twelve meters were two very different things.

And she wasn't sure which fall she was risking.

In the end, she didn't really have a choice. Kora made a low warning growl sound in the back of her throat, but too late. One of the cat things had found them, pouncing from out of the darkness to impact with the vine wall just to Lafayette's left. All the vines were shaking now.

And Lafayette's fingertips slipped free from their tenuous grasp on the vines. She was falling.

But before she could cry out—before she could quite process the thought that she was falling—she hit the ground.

She landed on her heels, but with too much impact to stay on her feet. She went spilling back into a bed of dried leaves and fallen vines. Not the world's softest mattress, but Lafayette was thankful for its presence all the same.

Or, at least, she *was*. Until she rolled awkwardly back onto her satchel.

And heard something crack.

"No," she said, even as she tried to catch the breath that her fall had just knocked out of her. "No, no, no."

"Lafayette!" Kora bellowed at her, digging her head under Lafayette's arm. As if the dog were even tall enough to get the girl back to her feet.

But it broke Lafayette's reverie. She scrambled to her feet even as two more cat things landed on the ground on either side of her.

Kora planted her front paws firmly and lowered her head, the growl in the back of her throat building to a threatening intensity.

The cats made sounds of their own as they circled around the girl and her dog. But they kept their distance.

Then Kora stopped growling, opening her mouth wide as if she were a dragon about to breathe fire. What came out of her mouth wasn't fire, though. It was a sound, a sound so high-pitched that Lafayette couldn't quite hear it.

Although the sudden pounding of a headache told her she hadn't imagined the sound.

The cats yowled in pain, not just the two in front of them, but at least a dozen more in the darkness of the tree branches all around them. Lafayette heard the sound of claws scratching on bark and leaves rustling madly as the cat things fled this surprising new source of agony.

Kora closed her mouth with a snap, then looked up at Lafayette.

"Right. Run," Lafayette agreed.

And the two of them sprinted off through the jungle.

Without the lantern, because that was still in the cell with her father.

Without her spare journal or his filled one, because those were with him as well.

Without a single example of any of the tablets, because all the ones that Lafayette had taken out of the classroom had ended up in that cell with her father.

But none of that mattered. Not compared to the one thing she was leaving behind that she knew she was going to need, the thing she knew she would miss forever.

Her father.

He just had to be running to catch up with her, Lafayette told herself again and again.

But her heart refused to believe it. If he were, she was sure she would sense it. She would feel it like she felt the presence of Kora beside her always, even though the jungle was often too dark for Lafayette to get more than the vaguest sense of the red dog's outline.

Then they were out of the tree cover, crossing the scree of rubble that led up to the rocky slope, up to the ridge above.

And Lafayette realized she had been feeling that rumble from the ship building for some time. It vibrated the ground she was running on, so softly at first that she hadn't really noticed it.

But she noticed it now. Maybe it was because she could see the sky ahead of her. More probably, it was because the moons above were reflecting off of the loose gravel all around her as she scrambled up the steep path.

That gravel was more than vibrating. It was moving. Entire waves of it were joining together to cascade down the slope.

Lafayette had to force her mind to stop picturing a massive boulder doing the same, coming down the hill from some unseen point just above her head.

She was so very tired.

But she didn't dare look back. Not even once. Not until she reached the campsite she had left behind so many days before.

She switched on the perimeter fence the instant she and Kora were inside of it, and almost wept in gratitude when it instantly came to steady green-lit life.

She was safe.

Even if the ground was still shaking.

Lafayette flopped down on the ground, and Kora pressed up close beside her.

And the two of them watched as an intense sphere of glowing blue light emanated from the jungle they had just left behind. That light looked like it was melting the trees, more and more of the sphere being exposed as more and more of the greenery grew thin and emaciated, then disappeared entirely.

The rumble was louder now, and the ground shaking was so severe that Lafayette found herself trying to clutch at the hard-packed dirt beside her hips. As if she needed to hold on to the planet to keep from falling off of it.

At least there were no more boulders above her. She was safe enough, for now.

But search as she might, there was no sign of her father emerging from the tree line to run to her. And as the light in the center of the crater grew brighter by the minute, there was no way she'd miss seeing him now.

If he were there.

Then the rumbling sound climbed in intensity to something too high-pitched to really be called a rumble anymore. And as much as Lafayette still felt it in her chest, the ground was no longer vibrating.

The air might be. It felt like it was. But the ground under her grasping hands had gone quite still.

Then the sphere of blue morphed into something almost arrow-shaped, shooting up into the sky so fast Lafayette's eyes could barely track it. It rose up and up, growing smaller as it got further away, until it was no larger than any of the other stars above. Although it was still brighter, and distinctly blue.

And then it arced off to the east and disappeared over the horizon.

Lafayette and Kora sat right where they were all through the rest of the night and past dawn of the next day.

But her father never joined them.

CHAPTER 26

Sameera's power supply had cracked in half. That was definitely the bad news.

But after a day of combing through all of her father's journals, Lafayette thought she knew of a way to… well, not exactly fix it.

No, what she found was a sliver of a hope. But it was a hope that refused to die.

It was the only hope she had. Her father was definitely gone. After another day of waiting, even she had to admit he wasn't on his way to her.

He was either dead in the jungle, caught up in that burning light before it had gone up into the sky.

Or he was still on the ship. The one that shone like a bright blue star, brighter than all the others. A star that moved from west to east, passing overhead three times at night.

She was pretty sure it was the latter. She had never believed that he would make it out to her, true. But now that she was without him, she couldn't stop believing that he was up there. In that ship.

Still alive.

Alive, but out of her reach to rescue him.

Sameera, on the other hand?

That shred of hope that Lafayette couldn't let go of was that she had figured out a way to keep Sameera with her.

She couldn't fix the power supply. That was true. It had cracked exactly in half. There was no putting that back together. Not without tools and knowledge she didn't have. And she doubted even Frank Paine could fix it if he were there. Some things just couldn't be repaired.

Without that massive power supply, Lafayette had nothing else powerful enough to allow Sameera's construct to make itself appear.

Lafayette was pretty sure she'd never see her beloved teacher again.

But she just might be able to hear her.

"You understand what I'm asking you, don't you, Kora?" she asked the dog, not for the first time. Or even the tenth.

"Lafayette," Kora said.

"You keep saying that, but I'm not sure you quite get it," Lafayette said. "If this works, Sameera will be there with you, in the part of your core that lets you say my name."

"Lafayette," Kora said.

"Right. But if this doesn't work—"

Lafayette choked on the next words. But she forced herself to say them out loud. Even though Kora wasn't really the one who needed to hear them.

That was Lafayette. Because thinking a thing in your head was one thing. Saying it out loud made it more real, somehow.

"Kora, I might break you," Lafayette said. Then she swiped at a tickle on her cheeks.

There were no bugs up on the ridge. But she kept that little fact far from the front of her brain.

Kora didn't say her name again. She just nuzzled her head under Lafayette's arm until she was resting it on Lafayette's lap. She scratched a paw against Lafayette's belly, a gesture she had always done to Momma when she wanted more attention.

Lafayette put both her hands on Kora's head and gave her ears the thorough scratching they deserved.

Then she swiped another tickle away from her own face with the back of her hand.

"Lafayette," Kora said as she sat up again. She was sitting tall, her chest thrust out, as if she were presenting her core to Lafayette.

"Right," Lafayette said, looking at the tiny green light that told her that Kora was okay. That she had plenty of power. That she could carry on for years and years in a way that the previous Kora hadn't been able to.

Lafayette really hoped she wasn't about to mess that up.

She looked at the parts she had removed from Sameera's core casing. She would keep all of it, of course. She would store it in the totes on the hover cart with the rest of her father's cherished artifacts.

But she couldn't fit the whole thing in Kora. Even with the juiced up hover disc taking the weight off her legs, Sameera's casing was just too bulky.

But Lafayette had examined all the parts carefully and had read the labels over and over until she was sure she knew what all the parts were.

There was only one part she'd need that was the most concentrated essence of Sameera.

And it was just small enough to fit beside Kora's own higher functions unit nestled beside her power supply.

"I have to turn you off," Lafayette said.

Kora said nothing. She just laid down on her left side and lifted her right legs up into the air.

And Lafayette turned the slider just by Kora's throat to the off position.

She opened the casing and found the connections she had known from her research of her father's journals would be there. She jacked Sameera's unit into Kora's unit, and then into the dog's power supply. Then she tucked everything in nice and tight, and closed the casing up again.

But her hand just hovered over that slider, not quite willing to commit to testing her work. She looked back over her shoulder, beyond the perimeter fence to the edge of the jungle below.

She scanned the tree line. But her father still wasn't there.

She turned back to the dog and flicked on the power.

Kora laid quietly for a dozen agonizing heartbeats as Lafayette held her breath, afraid to move, afraid to even think.

Then the dog's eyes blinked. She looked around as if seeing the world for the first time ever.

Which, maybe she was.

"Kora?" Lafayette asked.

"Lafayette," Kora said.

But she sounded different. She sounded like she knew that was only a name, not a word capable of conveying a thousand disparate meanings.

"Are you okay?" Lafayette asked her.

"Yes," she said, blinking again. Then she pushed herself to her feet and sat up to look at Lafayette.

"Yes?" Lafayette repeated, hardly daring to hope.

But hardly capable of not hoping.

"Yes," Kora said, a new brightness to her eyes. An intelligent brightness. "Oh, this is interesting."

"Do you know where you are?" Lafayette asked her.

"Do you mean on your world or do you mean in your dog?" Sameera asked.

Because it was definitely Sameera that was talking to her now.

"I'm so sorry I had to put you in there," Lafayette said.

"Because your father said my construct would be dangerous?"

"Well, that too. But mostly because when I was running away, I accidentally fell on your power supply and broke it. I didn't have a spare. But I could power just one small part of you inside of Kora. Is that okay? Or is this wrong?" Lafayette asked anxiously.

"This is marvelous," Sameera said. "Clever girl."

"So you feel okay being in there?" Lafayette asked.

"It feels different," Sameera said, looking down at herself, at her red paws and robotic chest.

"It's a different body. It will take a little getting used to, I suppose," Lafayette said.

"More than that, I'm afraid," Sameera said. "I'm not entirely myself in my own mind."

"What do you mean?" Lafayette asked, suddenly scared all over that she had messed something up.

"Well, Kora is still in here too," Sameera said. "I was going to say here in this head, only we're not inside the dog's head, are we?"

"I don't exactly understand what my father did," Lafayette admitted. "Kora's brain is still in her skull, so that's inside her head. But there is also something called a higher functions unit. That's also Kora, but it's inside her core. That's the part that lets her talk. But I think it still communicates with her brain somehow."

"And now those two things are communicating with a third, me," Sameera said.

"It's weird to watch," Lafayette said.

"It's very weird to feel," Sameera said.

"But you're okay?" Lafayette asked, still anxiously.

"I think so," Sameera said. But then she looked down at her paws again, almost gravely. "But I don't think I can quite call myself Sameera anymore. I'm feeling things, very strong drives, very strong emotions. Those are pure Kora, I'm sure. But I can't tune them out. They're a part of me now. I'm more than I was before, not less. But I'm still not sure that Sameera is who I am anymore."

"What do you want me to call you, then?" Lafayette asked.

"Well, Kora should be just fine," the dog said. "Yes, I feel a very strong response to that name. It's my name. Call me Kora."

"Kora," Lafayette said.

And Kora wagged her tail so hard she sent up a cloud of dust behind her.

"Lafayette," Kora said, but with a twinkle in her eye. Like they were sharing a little joke.

"The ship went up into the sky," Lafayette told her as she put the tools away, back inside her father's toolbox. "I've seen it go by at night. It's fast, but it seems to be moving at a steady speed now."

"It's in orbit then," Kora said, sounding pleased. "We did it." But then she looked around the camp and found the two of them were quite alone. "Your father?"

"I think he was on the ship when it went up into the sky," Lafayette said.

"I'm sure you're right," Kora said. "But you needn't worry. Even if Frank Paine can't find a way to get to him or to get him out of the brig, the cell will keep supplying him with food and water. It will keep him in top health."

"Yeah," Lafayette said glumly. "Maybe he can get one of the tablets I brought him working."

"Even if not, the ship is fully online by now," Kora said. "The panel in his cell might not let him out now that the emergency is over, but it will make sure he stays occupied. He speaks our language as well as you do now. He can interact with the panel. It will see to his needs."

"Yeah," Lafayette said, but no more cheered than before.

"What are you thinking?" Kora asked her.

"We have to get him back down," Lafayette said, making a fist with one hand. Not that she wanted to punch anything. It just felt like making a vow needed a gesture to show that she meant it. And this one felt right.

"How?" Kora asked.

"I don't know," Lafayette said. "But I know I'll figure it out."

"Someday," Kora said. That one word sounded less like a word of optimism and more like… well, almost a warning.

But Lafayette had no illusions about how hard her mission was going to be.

"Obviously we have to go to the capital first," she said. "We'll find my father's mentor and learn all that he knows. And then we'll find the clues my father hadn't followed up on yet, the trails he was still intending to follow, maybe hints that he hadn't ever uncovered. But one way or another, we'll find the remains of the other ships."

"That would be a start," Kora said. "I don't know anything at all about your world, so I don't really know how I'll be able to help you. Especially as I think I'll mostly have to pretend to just be your dog and not your friend and teacher. But I swear to you, Lafayette. I'll never leave your side."

"Same, Kora," Lafayette said, and threw her arms around the warmth of the dog, all fur and softly humming core.

Lafayette still felt the absence of her father like a physical ache. But she had felt that so many times before, all throughout her childhood.

At least this time she knew, he really couldn't get back to her. Not even if he wanted to.

But this time, she knew she could do what he couldn't.

She would find a way to get back to him.

And then they'd show their entire world the history that was all around them. The history that had been allowed to fall to the level of secrets and rumors.

Together, they would bring everything up into the light.

But the first steps of that journey, Lafayette would have to take alone.

Well, alone with Kora.

CHECK OUT BOOK TWO

History sleeps beneath them all, but only she sees it.

Lafayette Eloi grew up in a village of people who remained strangers to her. She and her mother always stood apart, separated from the others by their accent. By the secretive comings and goings of her wayward father. And by the forbidden knowledge her mother imparted to her in the dark of night.

With her mother dead and her father trapped in space, Lafayette finally learned why they kept that knowledge secret. Now the burden lies with her. She must protect it.

So Lafayette returns to the city where her parents first met. The city where they learned all that they passed on to her. The city where all the secrets still dwell, hidden in the shadows and under the ground.

And sometimes in plain sight.

But no one sees any of it. And Lafayette knows learning the why of that means unlocking the biggest secret of them all.

Plundering the Planetary Secrets (Available March 11, 2025 direct from me or April 15, 2025 in stores everywhere.)

SCI-FI SERIAL PODCAST!

Check out my new monthly podcast of serialized science fiction: THE TALES OF THE CHAI MAKHANI TRIO!

Elyot loathes the massive Commonwealth ships that hover menacingly over his home world of Adghal. He hates the Commonwealth enforcers who harass the populace even more. But with his mother missing and presumed dead, Elyot keeps his head down and strives to avoid notice. And he succeeds until the day two strangers enter his life...

New episodes of this sci-fi serial drop every 1st of the month.

Now streaming on Apple Podcasts, Google Podcasts, Spotify, Stitcher and more. Also available in eBook and print everywhere books or sold. For a complete episode listing, check out the page on my website.

COMPLETE SERIES: THE TRAVELS OF SCOUT SHANNON

The complete six-book series THE TRAVELS OF SCOUT SHANNON begin with book one, Under Falling Skies.

Scout Shannon's whole family died the day the Space Farers dropped an asteroid on their domed city. Now she lives alone, out in the wild with only her dogs for company. She prefers it that way.

But Scout finds herself at a crossroads. One road leads back to a quiet life snug under the protective dome of a city. The other road leads to a life in the rebellion, a life of adventure and excitement but also danger. Dare she try to find the rebels hiding in the hills?

Then a chance encounter with a stranger from the other side of the galaxy threatens to derail what remains of Scout's life. The entire galaxy awaits her, if she survives the next four days.

"Under Falling Skies", a young adult science fiction novel, set on a remote planet with a distinctly Old West feel. For fans of gunslinging women and young girl assassins. And dogs.

Under Falling Skies, the first book in THE TRAVELS OF SCOUT SHANNON, available everywhere now.

COMPLETE SERIES: THE RITCHIE AND FITZ SCI-FI MURDER MYSTERIES

The Ritchie and Fitz Sci-Fi Murder Mysteries starts with Murder on the Intergalactic Railway.

For Murdina Ritchie, acceptance at the Oymyakon Foreign Service Academy means one last chance at her dream of becoming a diplomat for the Union of Free Worlds. For Shackleton Fitz IV, it represents his last chance not to fail out of military service entirely.

Strange that fate should throw them together now, among the last group of students admitted after the start of the semester. They had once shared the strongest of friendships. But that all ended a long time ago.

But when an insufferable but politically important woman turns up murdered, the two agree to put their differences aside and work together to solve the case.

Because the murderer might strike again. But more importantly, solving a murder would just have to impress the dour colonel who clearly thinks neither of them belong at his academy.

Murder on the Intergalactic Railway, the first book in the Ritchie and Fitz Sci-Fi Murder Mysteries.

ALSO FROM KATE MACLEOD

Love heists and capers? Then check out my new series, THE VIC HARPER CAPERS. The action starts with the novella THE THIRD POLE JOB.

Vic Harper and her gang retired wealthy from their life of thievery and heists. Whether in a luxury condo overlooking the river in Minneapolis or in a modernist mansion built into the side of a mountain in Colorado, life comes easy now.

Perhaps too easy.

When an old friend asks for a favor his niece, Vic and her mentor Chase Woodward leap at the chance to relieve a little of the boredom. But a quick bit of B&E in a wealthy suburb of Chicago leads to an even greater challenge.

The prize? Nothing much. Just the opportunity to level a playing field for their friend's niece.

But the heist? May prove to be their toughest ever. Because to get to the prize, they'll have to climb a mountain.

And not just any mountain. Their prize waits on the summit of Mount Everest.

THE THIRD POLE JOB, the first novella in the Vic Harper Caper series. For those who love capers, heists and other impossible missions.

ALSO FROM RATATOSKR PRESS

Also from Ratatoskr Press, The Witches Three Cozy Mystery Series by Cate Martin, a mix of mystery and magic that begins with Book 1: Charm School.

Amanda Clarke thinks of herself as perfectly ordinary in every way. Just a small-town girl who serves breakfast all day in a little diner nestled next to the highway, nothing but dairy farms for miles around. She fits in there.

But then an old woman she never met dies, and Amanda was named in her will. Now Amanda packs a bag and heads to the big city, to Miss Zenobia Weekes' Charm School for Exceptional Young Ladies. And it's not in just any neighborhood. No, she finds herself on Summit Avenue in St. Paul, a street lined with gorgeous old houses, the former homes of lumber barons, railroad millionaires, even the writer F. Scott Fitzgerald. Why, Amanda can practically hear the jazz music still playing across the decades.

Scratch that. The music really, literally, still plays in the backyard of the charm school. Because the house stretches across time itself. Without a witch to protect this tear in the fabric of the world, anything can spill over. Like music.

Or like murder.

The complete series is out now, and it all starts with Charm School.

FREE EBOOK!

Like exclusive, free content?

To get two prequel short stories to THE RITCHIE AND FITZ SCI-FI MURDER MYSTERIES as well as a bonus prequel novelette to the completed six-book series THE TRAVELS OF SCOUT SHANNON, signup for my monthly newsletter at KateMacLeodWrites.com.

Thank you!

ABOUT THE AUTHOR

Kate MacLeod has written stories which have appeared in Analog, Strange Horizons and Mythic Delirium, among other places. She is also the author of two young adult science fictions series: The Travels of Scout Shannon, and The Ritchie and Fitz Sci-Fi Murder Mysteries. She also contributes to a serialized science fiction podcast called The Tales of the Chai Makhani Trio. She currently lives in Minneapolis, Minnesota.

Find out more about the author and sign up for her newsletter at KateMacLeodWrites.com.

ALSO BY KATE MACLEOD

Novels

The Slums of the Solar System:

Mitwa

The Mars of Malcontents

The Whole World for Each

Books 1-3 Box Set

The Travels of Scout Shannon:

Under Falling Skies

In Quaking Hills

Among Treacherous Stars

Against Impassable Barriers

Over Freezing Altitudes

At Galactic Central

The Travels of Scout Shannon Books 1-3

The Travels of Scout Shannon Books 4-6

The Travels of Scout Shannon Books 1-6

The Ritchie and Fitz Sci-Fi Murder Mysteries:

Murder on the Intergalactic Railway

Murder in the Skies

Body in the Catacombs

Death on the Summit

An Undiplomatic Murder

A Lethal Betrayal

The Forgotten Planet:

Raiding the Forgotten Derelict

Plundering the Planetary Secrets (Available March 11, 2025 direct from me or April 15, 2025 in stores everywhere.)

Sci-Fi Novellas

The Intergenerational Tree

I Rise into a Daybreak

Caper Novellas

The Third Pole Job

The Twelve Days of Christmas Job

10-Story Collections

Tales of Blood and Ink

Tales of Old Gods and New

5-Story Collections

Tales from Heian-Kyo and Others

Tales from the Edges and Ends

Tales from Forgotten Days

Tales from Ancient and Future Times